SHERLOCK

MYSTERY MAGAZINE

#12 (VOLUME 5 NUMBER 2)   March/April 2014

Sherlock Holmes Mystery Magazine #12 (Vol. 5, No. 2) is copyright © 2014 by Wildside Press LLC. All rights reserved. Visit us at wildsidemagazines.com.

SHERLOCK HOLMES AND IRENE ADLER
THE UNTOLD STORY

MARC BILGREY

" YOU DONT KNOW WHY IT'S OVER BETWEEN US?
YOU'RE SO CLUELESS. "

Publisher: John Betancourt
Editor: Marvin Kaye
Assistant Editors: Steve Coupe, Sam Cooper

Sherlock Holmes Mystery Magazine is published by Wildside Press, LLC. Single copies: $10.00 + $3.00 postage. U.S. subscriptions: $59.95 (postage paid) for the next 6 issues in the U.S.A., from: Wildside Press LLC, Subscription Dept. 9710 Traville Gateway Dr., #234; Rockville MD 20850. International subscriptions: see our web site at www.wildsidemagazines.com. Available as an ebook through all major ebook etailers, or our web site, www.wildsidemagazines.com.

The Sherlock Holmes characters created by Sir Arthur Conan Doyle are used by permission of Conan Doyle Estate Ltd., www.conandoyleestate.co.uk.

FROM WATSON'S SCRAPBOOK

On several occasions, I have been asked for my opinion about the BBC TV series, *Sherlock*, and what Holmes thinks of it. The answer to the latter is simple: my friend has never troubled himself to watch it, nor is he likely to do so. For my part, I have found the show mostly quite entertaining. Its relationship to the actual cases and events that Holmes and I participated in is, shall we say, remote? However, I put that consideration aside and enjoy it for what it is: a mixture of comedy[1], suspense, and rather clever ratiocination. I should also note that our friend, Inspector (retired) Lestrade, is quite fond of the actor who portrays him, one Rupert Graves.

My editorial colleague Mr Kaye and I discussed *Sherlock* and agreed to invite our friend and contributor Carole Buggé (also known as C E Lawrence) to give us her thoughts about the programme.

This issue contains no few than five of Holmes's adventures: my own "Adventure of the Blue Carbuncle," which is sometimes called my only Christmas story; the singular tale of Colonel Warburton's Madness, which I mentioned many years ago—a newcomer to our pages, Ms Sasscer Hill, successfully struggled with my scrawled notebook recounting of the case; Jack Grochot's "Disappearance of the Vatican Emissary," Martin Rosenstock's "Fool's Gold," and Gary Lovisi's "Challenger's Titanic Challenge."

---

1   *For instance, I find it quite amusing that they hired a decidedly slim, trim actor—Mark Gatiss, who is also a coproducer of the programme—to portray Holmes's brother Mycroft, who, I am sure you are aware is not at all slim or trim!*

A word about the later tale is in order. You are probably aware of the reputation of Professor George Edward Challenger, who went to a remote jungle and discovered prehistoric life in *The Lost World*, which my literary agent Conan Doyle shaped for publication. Two facts, however, are not well known concerning Challenger and Holmes: first, they are cousins, though the professor refuses to accept this as true, but Holmes assures me that it is so; this was first revealed by the scholar William S. Baring-Gould in his biographical study, *Sherlock Holmes of Baker Street*.

Secondly—and Challenger certainly was not aware of this!—during the "Lost World" expedition, the professor was accompanied by several individuals, including the renowned explorer Sir John Roxton. That worthy, however, yielded his place on the journey to Holmes, who disguised himself as Roxton. Details may be consulted in Mr Kaye's study, *The Histrionic Holmes*, which was published in the anthology, *The Game is Afoot*.

Now before I turn this forum over to Mr Kaye, I am pleased to inform you that Mrs Hudson has at long last returned to Baker Street, having arranged for permanent care for her ailing aunt. Holmes and I are frankly relieved to welcome her back, and celebrated her first evening home with dinner at her favourite restaurant.

—John H Watson, M D

I am pleased to welcome back two of our regular contributors: Hal Charles, with a new story about TV personality and detective Kelly Locke and her police inspector father Matthew; also, John Floyd's utterly charming Sheriff Lucy Valentine and her detectival mom Fran. British author Jay Carey also returns with a new story about her distaff sleuth, Detective Eureka Kilburn.

Appearing for the first time are Laird Long, who has submitted several examples of "flash fiction" to appear in future issues as well, and my dear friend Dianne Ell, who, incidentally first introduced me to Hal Charles. I first met Dianne before her marriage, when, as Dianne Neral, she studied mystery writing with me at New York University, and as a result, sold an excellent "big caper" novel, *The Exhibit*, now available from Amazon.com. For many years, Dianne did not do any writing, but I am pleased to announce that she has returned to the genre and *Sherlock Holmes Mystery Magazine* has bought two of her latest crime tales. Welcome back!!!!!

—Canonically Yours,
Marvin Kaye

COMING NEXT TIME...

**STORIES! ARTICLES!
SHERLOCK HOLMES & DR. WATSON!**

Sherlock Holmes Mystery Magazine #13
is just a few months away...watch for it!

Not a subscriber yet?
Send $59.95 for 6 issues (postage paid in the U.S.) to:

**Wildside Press LLC
Attn: Subscription Dept.
9710 Traville Gateway Dr. #234
Rockville MD 20850**

You can also subscribe online at
www.wildsidemagazines.com

SCREEN OF THE CRIME

by Lenny Picker

"THE SCARLET CLAW": AN APPRECIATION

"There is nothing new under the sun. It has all been done before."

That's Holmes himself, in his first recorded outing, *A Study in Scarlet*. The Master made this observation to Tobias Gregson, remarking that the state of the corpse he was observing put him in mind of "the death of Van Jansen, in Utrecht, in the year '34." But the citation of Ecclesiastes could also apply to two of the hottest media adaptations of Holmes and Watson in decades—BBC's *Sherlock* and CBS's *Elementary*. In very different ways, both series place the pair in modern times—in London and New York City, respectively.

In discussing the origins of *Sherlock*, with Al Jazeera America, co-creator Steven Moffat cited an unexpected inspiration for him and partner Mark Gatiss:

> And we started talking about all the various films—and there are those films with Basil Rathbone and Nigel Bruce that are updated to the 1940s—and we sort of haltingly admitted to each other that somehow, in some strange magic way, mad and cheaply-made though they are, they somehow caught more of

Sherlock Holmes than many of the more serious adaptations. And the very obvious step—that's updated to the 1940's, just a different period piece, as far as we're concerned—we sort of started to speculate: 'Is someone going to do that again for Sherlock Holmes? Update it to the modern day?' And of course we just started thinking: 'It should be us! We'll be so cross if it's not us!'

I, too, was first exposed to Holmes in other media via the Rathbone/Bruce films. The first two, 1939's *The Hound of the Baskervilles* and *The Adventures of Sherlock Holmes*, were set in period; the first, a straightforward and solid adaptation of the Canon's best-known, and most-filmed tale, the second, a thrilling and credible duel with the Napoleon of Crime himself. But the studio that made those two, Twentieth Century Fox, stopped there.

Fortunately for lovers of the actors in those roles, Universal Pictures signed them up for a further twelve films, released between 1942 and 1946. As Moffat noted, this Baker Street dozen was not set in a world of hansom cabs and telegrams, but in the World War II and post-World War II era. The rationale for the update (the term reboot was decades away) was provided in a title card right after the opening credits of the first Universal Holmes, *Sherlock Holmes and the Voice of Terror*. Before plunging the viewer into a plot allegedly based on "His Last Bow," and the series's Holmes vs. the Nazis trilogy (which also included 1943's *Sherlock Holmes and the Secret Weapon* and *Sherlock Holmes in Washington*), the filmmakers conveyed the following message:

> "Sherlock Holmes, the immortal character of fiction created by Sir Arthur Conan Doyle, is ageless, invincible and unchanging. In solving significant problems of the present day he remains—as ever—the supreme master of deductive reasoning."

Despite this, action often trumped deduction in the first three modern Rathbone/Bruce Holmes films, and had the series continued in this vein, it would not have the place in as many Sherlockians's hearts as it does. But the fourth film, 1943's *Sherlock Holmes Faces Death*, which borrowed heavily from "The Musgrave Ritual," changed direction. Solving multiple murders, not saving England from Germany, became the welcome focus.

Of the last Universal nine, there's a wide consensus as to the best, an opinion I concur with. In fact, 1944's *The Scarlet Claw* is one of my top ten Holmes movies of all time, richly-atmospheric, well-plotted, and suspenseful.

> SPOILER ALERT—this column will discuss the plot and solution of *The Scarlet Claw* in some detail, so, if you haven't seen it, stop reading, and spend 74 minutes watching it (it's available online). I'll still be here when you get back. And don't look at the lurid film poster, which gives too much away after its promises of "New Thrills! New Terror!"

Everybody here now? Good.

The film's opening is one of the most effective in any Holmes film. A church-bell tolls as the camera pans over a bleak and fog-shrouded landscape. As the tocsin continues (it will sound ominously in the background for a few minutes), the scene shifts to the village of La Morte Rouge (literally, The Red Death), and the interior of Journet's inn, whose silent occupants look around in fear. Mr. Potts, the local postman, enters, and a minute-plus into the movie, speaks the first line of dialogue; Potts asks what everyone at Journet's is wondering—"Who could be ringing the church bell at this time?" Potts goes on to speculate that a "what" rather than a "who" might be responsible, prompting the inn's owner, Emil Journet, to link the sound with a recent attack that left a farmer's sheep dead, with their throats ripped out—but without leaving any tracks. Potts adds to the spookiness by reporting that another local saw a "weird glow moving across the marshes" on the previous night, and even more mangled livestock were discovered in its wake.

It's hard not to be reminded of *The Hound of The Baskervilles* from the outset, with these intimations of a supernatural explanation for the goings-on, and a mysterious beast with a taste for ripped-out throats. And there are certainly worse templates for an original screenplay—while *Hound* remains the benchmark, some of the best novel pastiches have set Holmes against a mystery seemingly incapable of a rational explanation. (See my previous column on pastiches that deserve filming in *SHMM 10*.)

And paralleling the opening of the 1939 Rathbone *Hound*, which starts with Sir Charles running for his life while a hound bays in the background, a body is found in short order—the corpse of Lady Lillian Penrose, clutching the bell-rope, with her throat torn out as if by an animal's claw. (Repeat viewings invariably reveal some loose ends—it's unlikely that a woman with such wounds would have the strength to crawl to the church and pull the bell-rope for several minutes—but that's almost churlish quibbling under the circumstances, as the plotting is generally very tight). Word of her death reaches her husband, who is presiding over a meeting of the Royal Canadian Occult Society in Quebec; fortuitously, if somewhat improbably, the society's meeting is attended by Holmes and Watson (it's hard to believe that they'd cross the pond just for the meeting, and there's no basis for believing that this all happens right after *Sherlock Holmes in Washington*).

The setup pits Holmes against the believers in the irrational from the very beginning; in a nicely-Canonical line, Holmes observes, "Facts are always convincing, Lord Penrose. It is the conclusions drawn from the facts that are frequently in error." Lord Penrose counters with what he considers "facts"—an account of attacks a century earlier in Le Morte Rouge which parallel the current depredations (as with the Hugo Baskerville legend, there's a considerable gap between the appearances of the beast) that left three people dead, with their throats torn out, following reports of an apparition on the marshes. Holmes is not close-minded, but he notes that there are alternate explanations for the deaths, and thus the occurrences cannot be regarded as conclusive proofs of the existence of the supernatural, "without further data."

Before the debate can continue, word reaches Penrose of his wife's death. He rushes home, to be followed a day later by the Baker Street duo. Tragically, a letter from Lady Penrose seeking Holmes's help arrives after her death; she wrote him, "I have every reason to believe that my life is in danger. Yet, if you were to ask me how I know, I couldn't give you a logical answer. There's nothing tangible, just a terrible premonition. It is all so frightfully real."

Holmes accepts the commission from the dead woman to find her murderer, telling Watson that "for the first time, we've been retained by a corpse." This added wrinkle—a lesser writer would simply have Holmes choose to investigate on his own—lends another layer of creepiness to what is one of the darkest Holmes movies—a later murder is genuinely heart-breaking. And the message from beyond the grave, with its fear of something intangible, is also a good fit for a storyline where there is ostensibly a supernatural evil force at work. Holmes speculates that Lady Penrose was in fear of the consequences of a dark secret from her past, but that guess (yes, Holmes does guess—"And now tell me the result of your visit to Mrs. Laura Lyons—it was not difficult for me to guess that it was to see her that you had gone") seems off; had she believed that a past sin was coming home to roost, why characterize her fear as intangible?

Over the new widower's objections, Holmes and Watson examine the corpse, getting vital, first-hand insights into the wounds, which allow Holmes to theorize that a human could have inflicted them. (And the tool he suspects is responsible, a five-prong garden weeder, is similar to the weapon in one of the best pastiches pitting Holmes against a werewolf.) In a line which would have made spiritualist Conan Doyle happy, Holmes tells Penrose, who does not welcome his presence or his intentions, that he "neither believes nor disbelieves in anything, including psychic phenomena."

Holmes realizes that in a prior life Lady Penrose was a famous actress, Lillian Gentry, and uses that fact to begin an earth-bound investigation into those who had a motive to kill her. He has an encounter with the local monster himself; having convinced Watson he was elsewhere (asleep in bed), in another *Hound* parallel, he goes on the marshes, and in a very effective scene, enhanced by ominous background music, is stalked by a glowing figure of a man, as the church-bell again tolls at an odd hour, freaking out the regulars at Journet.

> (*RENEWED SPOILER ALERT*—thus far, I've covered the first half-hour or so of the film, so if you haven't watched it, please do yourself a favor and do so.)

Against viewer expectations, the script has the monster explained halfway through; it is a human wearing clothing coated with Stapleton's favorite chemical, phosphorus—and Holmes even identifies the man in the costume, a local named Tanner. But with so much of the running time left, it's no surprise that Tanner's apparent death doesn't wrap everything up; Holmes deduces that

Tanner, like the monster, is merely a cover identity for a clever murderer, one who strikes successfully two more times, despite Holmes's best efforts to foil him. The climax again copies *Hound*—Holmes gets word out that he and Watson are leaving town, and sets up the killer's expected next victim as bait.

The solution—the murderer, an insane actor who had an unrequited passion for Lillian Gentry, was also posing as Potts the postman—is brilliant; Watson had earlier cited a classic short mystery in which the postman was the killer, "invisible" by virtue of his pedestrian routine—a nice bit of misdirection. Potts has been a likeable eccentric, but he is also, in retrospect, someone without an alibi—he enters the tavern at the outset after the bell began tolling; and he's also one of those who talks up the monster. Pretty much everything works here—the creepy storyline, the rural Canadian setting, the false ending, the depiction of Holmes's fallibility, and his ultimate success in unmasking a particularly vicious and crafty killer. If there is one major drawback, it is the continued scripting of Watson as a bumbling, if endearing, idiot—he blithers, is preoccupied with his stomach, mutters semi-coherently under his breath, and falls into a bog twice. Rathbone makes Holmes's affection for Watson convincing, but as noted by others, it's a stretch to think that such a boob would not have driven the Canonical Holmes to a 14% solution, or stronger.

Of all the Rathbone films, this is one that most, in my opinion, calls out for a remake, one where improved special effects can make the monster of Le Morte Rouge even scarier, and where a more effective Watson can reinforce the tragic nature of the murders, rather than serving as cheap comic relief.

✗

Lenny Picker, who has not yet fallen into a bog, can be reached at lpicker613@gmail.com.

ASK MRS HUDSON

by Mrs Martha Hudson

Dear Mrs Hudson,

You have been kind enough to share your experiences with Mr Sherlock Holmes, but I am curious about the good Doctor. Is Dr Watson one of those very neat and tidy ex-military men?

Very truly yours,

Enquiring in Edinburgh

✗   ✗   ✗   ✗

Dear Enquiring,

Doctor Watson is a kind and generous soul, but I speak with authority when I write that neatness and order are not appreciable parts of his character, at least regarding his domestic arrangements. To be perfectly honest, which I always endeavour to be, even if he were of such a disposition, a week in the company of Mr Holmes would either break him of the habit or send him into the streets, clutching his hair and tearing his clothes in despair.

Both Mr Holmes and Dr Watson are excellent tenants in many ways. Please do not take my comments regarding their personal habits as a condemnation of them as gentlemen, for they are generally thoughtful (the Doctor moreso than Mr Holmes), undemanding, and promptly settle their accounts (in this case, Dr Watson occasionally falls behind Mr Holmes, most frequently during the racing season). However, their favourable traits end decisively when speaking of neatness and order. Many is the time the girl and I would enter their chambers, intent upon cleaning the hearth or clearing away the breakfast dishes, only to have Mr Holmes leap up from his chemical apparatus and forbid us entry because he is at a delicate moment in his experiment, or peer at us from a seat on the carpet, surrounded by swaths of paper, and request that we quickly exit and close the door behind us, for he is conducting research and cannot be disturbed. It is true that Dr Watson does not actively object to our cleaning the rooms, but he certainly does not appear to take any part in maintaining any semblance of order in those selfsame rooms.

I am certain the good Doctor would not object to my confiding to my readers that his bedchamber is less untidy than the parlour for the reason that he keeps very little there, save his clothing. He has the generally masculine habit of draping various pieces of clothing over any convenient surface, so I will find cravats over the back of his chair, collars on the washstand, and once I even discovered his waistcoat hanging from the gas fixture!

Despite my complaints, I would be very distressed to see either of my gentlemen leave. They might not be perfect tenants, but one is never bored with them around.

Yours,

Mrs Hudson

✗　✗　✗　✗

Dear Mrs Hudson,

We often read of Mr Holmes donning a disguise for a case. Do you help him clean and organize all the various costumes for his disguises? When he is disguised as a woman, where does he purchase women's clothing large enough to fit a tall man?

Humbly yours,

Wondering in the West End

✗　✗　✗　✗

Dear Wondering,

In general, the types of disguises that Mr Holmes assumes need little in the way of cleaning or maintenance. In other words, they gain verisimilitude from a certain amount of filth and wear. For those which do require cleaning, either the girl or I will give them a good brush and mend any small tears, or we will send them out to be laundered with the rest of the household linen. Mr Holmes keeps a certain number of these disguises in his chambers, but as far as I can see, there is absolutely no organizing principle for them, and he had forbidden me to 'meddle with his things.' How he manages to find anything is still a mystery to me.

Suitable women's clothing may be acquired in a number of ways, including having private fittings with a discreet seamstress (we know several whose discretion is legendary), purchasing used clothing in a variety of shops, or combing through donations to a mission or other charitable organization. A thrifty housekeeper is able to alter a dress to accommodate a taller figure by letting out hems or adding a contrasting strip of fabric to the bottom of the skirt. Shawls or loose jackets may be used to cover up any little difficulties one may have with loosening fitted bodices or shoulder seams. Of course, in Mr Holmes's case, he is an excellent actor and can contrive to appear to lose several inches in height when necessary, so although he is indeed a tall man, he does not necessarily seem so when assuming the character of a woman or small man.

Yours very truly,

Mrs Hudson

⚹   ⚹   ⚹   ⚹

Dear Mrs Hudson,

I have thoroughly enjoyed reading about Mr Holmes's thrilling adventures, and yet would be loath to actually experience the dangers encountered by both Mr Holmes and Dr Watson. In several cases, the dangers did not stop at your front door. Are you ever frightened of Mr Holmes's clients?

Your obedient servant,

Frightened in Finchley

⚹   ⚹   ⚹   ⚹

Dear Frightened,

It would be foolish and vainglorious of me to boast that I have never been frightened by one of Mr Holmes's clients. In fact, there were a number of times when there was such a commotion coming from Mr Holmes's chambers that I was near to sending Billy out to fetch a constable.

Occasionally, when Mr Holmes is not at home and a dubious person has called, Billy and I have taken a more active part in protecting ourselves and Mr Holmes. I particularly recall one day, when Mr Holmes was out investigating a robbery. I was in the front hall when there was a peremptory knock at the door. When Billy opened the door, in rushed a greasy weasel of a man, followed by another, so broad of shoulder he almost had to turn sideways to enter, and so bulging with muscle it was a wonder he managed to find a decent tailor.

'Where is Mister Sherlock Holmes,' cried the small man, his accent pure and refined. I could scarcely believe so unprepossessing a person could speak so. 'Where is the blackguard?'

'He is not at home, sir,' said I, registering as much disapproval as I could. 'If you would care to leave a card, I will ensure he receives it upon his return.' No matter how refined his accent, I would not allow anyone who dared to call my boarder a blackguard into Mr Holmes's chambers.

'Leave a card?' He turned toward the stair. 'No, that will not do! I know the scoundrel has my papers, and by Gad [*Pray excuse the term, but I endeavour to be honest in my reporting, even at the risk of shocking my readers. —Mrs H.*] I will find them if I have to tear his rooms to pieces!'

Before he could mount the stair, Billy grabbed an umbrella from the stand and leapt onto the treads, holding the umbrella before him as one would a rapier. (Mr Holmes had recently been instructing Billy and several other boys in the fine art of fencing, and I was pleased that Billy decided this was the perfect time to practice.)

'Back, sir! Back!' Billy brandished the umbrella.

The man reared back, smacking into his large companion. 'You young—'

'Have a care, sir!' I cried, snatching up another umbrella and, since I have never received instruction on how to wield a sword or rapier, I assumed a combative stance and held it in both hands, as if it were a cudgel. 'Leave at once or I shall call for the constable!' I believe my voice wavered only slightly.

At that, the large man began to laugh, slapping his massive knee and wiping the tears from his eyes.

'Well, Reggie, I believe you must concede the field to Mr Holmes's valiant defenders.' His gaze traveled from Billy to me, and his shoulders shook with his chuckles.

The small man frowned as he exchanged a glance with his companion. 'But Bert, I must have those papers!' His voice took on a keening quality, very like that of a young child who has been told to put away his toys and prepare for bed.

'So leave your card and we'll return to discuss this with Mr Holmes when he's at home. From what I have heard, he's a reasonable man who might be open to negotiation.'

For a moment, I thought that 'Reggie' would continue to argue, but he suddenly bowed his head and sighed. 'Very well. Please give this to Mr Holmes.' He extracted a calling card from his pocket and laid it on the coat stand.

With a brief, rather shamefaced apology for disturbing us, both men hurriedly left, and Billy clattered down the stair to shut the door behind them. I collected the umbrellas and returned them to the stand, then picked up the card.

Well, dear readers! I must not mention names, especially names so readily recognized by the general public, but rest assured that Mr Holmes came to an understanding with 'Reggie' and 'Bert.' Papers were returned, and Billy and I both received a handsome apology for the invasion, as well as a generous *pour boire.*

Afterward, Mr Holmes did offer to give me a few fencing lessons; I politely declined.

Very truly yours,
Mrs Hudson

A SCANDAL IN BO MEDIA

by Hal Charles

I

As the elevator rocketed toward the penthouse, Kelly Locke couldn't decide if she were more nervous or curious. In the fifteen years she had worked for Channel 4, first as a reporter, then as a news anchor, she had never been invited to the office of the TV station's owner. She had met Bruce Count at the office holiday parties, even used his lavish suite at the stadium, but being summoned to his office immediately after *The Six O'Clock News* was a first.

As the elevator arrived at her destination, she buttoned her short jacket and ran her fingers through her Katie Couric-styled auburn hair. The door opened to reveal a handsome, middle-aged man in a dark suit and club tie, which suggested to Kelly her boss was matching her professionalism.

"Really insightful interview with our senator on the news tonight," he said. "How did you get him to reveal his views on Social Security reform?"

"The senator and I are old friends. I did him a favor a few years ago."

"Hope it didn't compromise your journalistic integrity." Count smiled warmly at her.

"Hardly. He's part of a golf foursome with my father, and I merely partnered with him."

"And they beat us by twelve strokes," boomed a familiar voice from behind her host.

"Dad," Kelly said, greeting the city's Chief of Detectives, "what are you doing here?"

"Actually," said Bruce Count, "you wouldn't be here tonight if it weren't for your P. R. rep...I mean, your father."

"I have to admit I'm intrigued," she said, giving her dad a hug.

"Let's go into my study," said the CEO.

When they had seated themselves in plush leather chairs, a butler brought them monogrammed glasses of cognac.

"Don't worry," said the CEO. "I caught your series last week on the dangers of second-hand smoke, but"—he said with a laugh—"you're welcome to use a meerschaum pipe."

Her father almost spit out his drink.

"Who," continued the CEO, "doesn't know of your off-air avocation of private investigation with your partner, Dr. Watson…I mean, Detective Locke."

"Bruce contacted me a few days ago, and I assured him the stories were all true and that you are indeed the reincarnation of a fictional detective. I filled him in about some recent cases—that business with the jewelry store, the adventure at my high school reunion—"

"And even that birthday party your father threw for you," concluded her host. "Now don't keep me hanging. Aren't you going to look at my clothes and tell me where I've been today?"

"That's easy. You've stayed in your penthouse office all day," said Kelly. "Rumor has it you rarely leave."

"And do you as a veteran reporter subscribe to rumors?" asked her boss.

"No, but I do follow you on Twitter."

"Touché," he said, pressing a remote and starting a blazing fire. "Now that we've established your extraordinary credentials, I need to tell you the specific reason I invited you up tonight."

‖

Over the hiss of the gas logs, Kelly could hear the late March winds assaulting the CEO's citadel. Bruce Count picked up a gilded picture frame from the oak mantel. "Do you know why this news corporation is technically known as BO Media?"

"No," said Matt Locke. "I don't believe I do."

Smoothing her dark skirt, Kelly said, "I'm pretty sure the 'B' stands for Bruce and the 'O' is for your business partner, who is—"

"Olivia, my wife. When Flaubert proclaimed the ideal narrator of fiction as 'everywhere present, but nowhere visible,' he might have been describing my young wife."

Kelly remembered how after Olivia's being a no-show at the last Christmas party, the water cooler chatter centered on why she never appeared at public functions. One reveler had even suggested jestingly, 'It's as if he killed her.' Or, suggested another, 'She's just a figment of his imagination.' "I'm sorry," Kelly said, "but I've never met her."

"Almost nobody has. Olivia, I'm afraid, is painfully, perhaps neurotically shy. She loves her charity work, but prefers to be the great invisible hand. I'm sure it has something to do with the untimely death of her father and the inheritance of all that money at such a young age, but that's between her and her well-paid psychiatrist."

"Before coming here tonight, I tried to find a picture of her in our files or on the Internet," Kelly's father admitted, "but I turned up zippo."

"Like Greta Garbo, my wife wants to be alone in her little room above us now. She calls it her aerie. In fact, I think that aside from Dr. Carpenter, her shrink, I'm the only person she allows within gun range."

Kelly noted the odd metaphor.

Count sat down slowly. "I once was a venture capitalist with a good idea for a media company, but if it weren't for Olivia's capital I might still be venturing. And"—he paused dramatically—"that could still happen…without your help."

Kelly said, "You sound like you're about to lose her."

"I might," said the CEO. He carefully set his wife's picture on the mantle beside a bronze statue of Neptune taming a seahorse. "There's no way to say what I'm about to, so I'll dive right in. Do you know who Abby Addison is?"

"Our city's version of Kim Kardashian," said Kelly. "She's famous for being famous."

"And for being a big pain in the patootie," said her father. "She's always complaining to the mayor we don't provide her enough protection when she's the one creating the crowds that necessitate protection."

"I wish somebody had protected me from her," said Bruce Count ruefully. "About a year ago I committed…let's call it an 'indiscretion' with her."

"If the papers are to be believed," said Kelly, "you and a lot of the city's males."

"That, however," said the CEO, doesn't excuse my 'indiscretion.' In all the years we have been married I promise you I have cheated on my wife only this once."

"Have you told Olivia?" broached Matt Locke.

"That would be the equivalent of pushing her off her aerie's balcony. I cannot let her under any circumstances discover what I have done."

"If she's this isolated," Kelly posed, "how is she to find out?"

"That's just it. Abby has threatened to expose me to my wife in two days on our tenth anniversary…"

"You're being blackmailed," Kelly concluded.

"The good reporter that you are," said Bruce Count, "you have just answered a question posed by some of the city's less reputable news sources—how does Abby Addison maintain such a high style of living when she has no apparent means of support?"

"Blackmail R Us," said Matt Locke.

"I'm afraid I'm not the only male in this city who has been put in such a compromising position," said the CEO. "Abby's parents died and left her destitute she told me, but she vowed she would always enjoy the highlife."

"Would you like me to arrest her?" asked Matt Locke.

"On what count?" said the CEO. "I have no evidence, just the memory of someone whispering in my ear last week while I was having lunch downtown of what my 'indiscretion' would cost."

"Abby," said the Chief of Detectives.

"I'm just lucky no paparazzi caught that," said Bruce Count. "You see, there can't be even a whiff of a scandal."

"How much does she want?" said Kelly.

"One million in cash," said Count.

"And for that what do you get?" pressed Matt Locke.

"The only record of my 'indiscretion'." Count dusted off the statue with his handkerchief. "Of course, I can easily afford that."

"But what you're afraid of," Kelly figured out, "is that because she knows how much you fear exposure, she'll keep coming back to that well."

"I don't know how many married men can honestly say this," said Count, "but I truly love my wife and will do anything to prevent her from being hurt."

And probably losing the financial underpinning of BO Media, thought Kelly. "So what would you like us to do?"

"Why, why," stammered the CEO, "recover the evidence and prevent this new breed of venture capitalist from ever being able to harm my wife."

"Why us?" said Kelly. "The city has plenty of investigators… and worse."

"I want someone with as much scruples as sense…somebody I can trust…somebody to make sure no hint of this impropriety takes wing. Obviously both of your credentials are impeccable."

"When do we start?" said Kelly.

III

Kelly stood before the roaring fire. "My first thought was to try to get the evidence back from Miss Addison, but we don't live in the 19th century with its limited amount of places to conceal the goods."

"According to her," said the CEO, "the evidence is a video of our *pas de deux*."

"You were honey-trapped," said Matt Locke.

"And lucky the world isn't watching you on YouTube right this minute," added Kelly.

"Which Miss Addison could still do if I haven't paid her in two days or recovered the evidence," said Count.

"Our advantage," said Kelly, "is your wife's very isolation."

"How so?" said the CEO.

"To carry through on her threat," Kelly elaborated, "Abby Addison would have to get the evidence to Olivia. You could, however, screen all her mail, packages, and visitors."

"Couldn't our adventuress just call your wife?" said Matt Locke.

"My wife does not take calls. In fact, she's one of the few women in this country who doesn't even own a cell."

Matt Locke persisted. "Addison could announce it on TV or the Internet."

"My wife does not watch TV and has no idea what the Internet is."

"Addison could hire a crop duster to tow around a banner or a blimp to show it on its side."

"But with your contacts," said the CEO, buying into Kelly's idea of splendid isolationism, "you could probably get Homeland Security to ground all such aircraft."

"*Parkour*," said Matt Locke desperately. "You know, those urban acrobats who think every city building is a starter course for K2."

"I'm sure a security guard or two with a rifle could discourage that kind of social climbing," said the CEO. "But Abby's nothing if she's not innovative. With the high rises surrounding this building, she could probably project an image on the side of one that would be visible from Olivia's apartment."

Matt Locke stroked his chin. "Even Abby doesn't have the juice or the funds necessary to secure and set up the projection equipment needed for such an undertaking in the middle of town."

Kelly chuckled to herself as she sensed her father and her boss were engaged in a contest of one-upmanship—who could come up with the weirdest ploy for getting the damning video to Olivia.

"What about some sort of remote-controlled glider or plane to fly into the window?" pressed the CEO.

Why not steal a military drone, thought Kelly.

"You know," said Matt Locke, "not all drones are Predators. I bet—"

"The building is climate-controlled with sealed windows and hurricane-proof glass," countered Count with a tone of victory.

"The more I think about it," said Kelly, having enough of their absurd duel. "There's a fundamental flaw in this isolationist's approach—time. She can outwait us. And sooner or later when your wife goes out for something as simple as a trip to her psychiatrist, a desire to vote, an annual checkup, she'll strike."

"Then what do we do?" said Matt Locke.

"I think with my isolationism approach I was on the right track," said Kelly. "I just need a little perception shift."

IV

The next night during *The Six O' Clock News* Kelly waited patiently while her co-host, Chuck Mann, droned on about how many franks he had downed at the ballpark that afternoon. Her eyes were patiently glued to "Professor Backwards," the clock that was suspended below the lens of camera one and ran in reverse to inform them how much time remained before the cut-away to network news.

When the clock indicated 01:00, Kelly turned to her co-host and interrupted him with a quip. "Gee, Chuck, I wonder who the real hot dog is in that story." Then, staring intently into her camera, she said, "On a serious note, I would like to make an important personal announcement. As tomorrow is our tenth anniversary, I want to publically declare something that we have kept private for all these years because we didn't want it to look like I had advanced from beat reporter to news anchor at the city's largest station through nepotism. After ten years I think I have established solid credentials on my own."

"Nepotism?" said Chuck Mann skeptically. "You're related to someone here? Don't tell me you're really Bruce Count's long-lost daughter?"

"Nope. I can't, but I can tell you that the woman you've been hitting on every night the past few years is really Olivia, the wife of your boss, Bruce Count."

As the newscast faded to network, Chuck Mann looked like he was going to throw up every one of his hotdogs.

V

The next day Kelly chose to lunch at the very public Baker Street Pub, a trendy bistro in the ground floor of the BO Media Building. She was staring at the reproduction of a Sidney Paget illustration of the Great Detective entering his abode when someone sat down at the table across from her. The figure was dressed in a gray pin-stripe suit complete with a navy-blue club tie and bowler. Despite the short haircut, Kelly could tell her "guest" was a woman.

"So you are actually the elusive Olivia," said the woman across the table.

"Guilty," said Kelly, "and you are...?"

"A person I promise you will never see again. I have been looking for you, and now that I have found you, I would like to present you with a gift." She pushed a small box that resembled a jeweler's case across the table.

"But we hardly know each other," said Kelly, taking the box in hand. "What is it?"

"A jump-drive complete with a short action movie."

"I'm afraid I can't pay you for it," said Kelly, "or the sequel."

"I'm not asking for payment," said the figure, "and there will be neither sequels nor copies. This is a one-of-a-kind *objet d'art*."

"To guarantee its uniqueness," Kelly said matter-of-factly, "I have taken the liberty to have my personal photographer record this entire transaction." She glanced over her shoulder to a table in the back to indicate where her cameraman was indeed recording everything.

The figure stood up, seemingly a bit confused. "It doesn't matter. I am true to my word. While you will never see me again and I have given away my only copy," she said, flashing just the hint of a smile, "I will always have the satisfaction of knowing that you will have to look at what I have given you and that I will indeed have kept my promise to a dear friend, your husband."

"And, Miss Addison," said Kelly, "should you violate your word, I will be forced to turn over my cameraman's footage to Matthew Locke, the city's Chief of Detectives, who will arrest you for blackmail."

VI

That evening Kelly concluded *The Six O'Clock News* by admitting to her hoax of claiming to be Olivia Count.

"But why?" asked a confused Chuck Mann.

"Yesterday," Kelly reminded him, "was April Fools' Day."

Chuck Mann had a look on his face, Kelly thought, as if he had just discovered fire.

VII

Immediately after the newscast, Kelly met her father and her boss in the penthouse. She handed the jump-drive to the CEO, assuring him, "I am certain it's the only record of your indiscretion."

"You rushed out of here so fast the other night," said Matt Locke. "What did you mean by perception shift?"

"We were playing defense against Abby Addison, and, Dad, how many times have you told me the best defense is a good offense?"

"I saw that," said Count. "I was confused by your surprise announcement on the news last night. I've spent the day telling reporters 'No comment'."

"I didn't know what exactly you were doing, honey," said her father, "but since I trust you, I convinced your boss to be non-committal."

"I…I cannot thank you enough," said Count. "You are even better than your reputation. In fact, it almost makes me wish you *were* Olivia."

"Careful," warned Kelly. "You've already been too far down that road once."

"And, believe me," said Count, "once is enough. And about the real Olivia, you might say she is *the* woman for me."

✗

CHALLENGER'S TITANIC CHALLENGE

by Gary Lovisi

CHALLENGE BEGINS:

McArdle had Malone on the ropes once again. This time, sending his young reporter to visit the man he called "the angry brute" because of their previous Maple White Land adventure. Malone had written that up in a series of articles in *The Chronicle* last year under the title *The Lost World*—now the thought of facing that most difficult of men once again was certainly daunting. For the world was coming upon the one-year anniversary of the *Titanic* tragedy. The ship had gone down in icy north Atlantic waters with approximately 1,500 passengers and crew lost. McArdle wanted a feature article on the reason behind the sinking of that most "unsinkable" of great ocean liners upon its maiden voyage after hitting an iceberg the night of April 14, 1912.

Now, one year later, Malone was to visit Professor George Edward Challenger once again. His mission this time to challenge Challenger, England's foremost scientific mind, to obtain his very particular theory upon the scientific reason behind the sinking. Malone was sure he was in for a most difficult and unusual situation, surely nothing he could have expected, and the Professor would once again prove him correct. So Malone set off to see Challenger and accept what fury would come.

"I must admit that I am rather incompetent in this area," Malone candidly told the Professor upon his visit to his home at Enmore Park. He was a newspaper reporter, and a good one—but certainly no scientist.

Challenger smiled indulgently, "Why, that is the most incisive comment you have made since I have known you, Malone. I am gratified when the incompetent admit their incompetence and acknowledge the superior intellect of a truly first class mind."

"Which, of course, you possess in avid abundance," Malone dared reply, but it was in all seriousness, for he took care not to show the least bit of criticism, since he was well aware of the Professor's volatile personality.

"Certainly, young man," Challenger boomed in a blustery voice, pointing his huge black beard at his guest when he lifted his head as if it were a weapon. "So what is it you want to know? Not another article for your Fleet Street rag, I pray."

Malone swallowed hard, for he had come to Challenger precisely for that very reason, which he knew would surely cause the stunted Hercules before him to explode into anger and blind rage. Rage that could end in violence. The two men had come to blows once before. Two years previously, upon the beginning of their Lost World adventure it had happened, but then Challenger's wife intervened and thankfully saved Malone from her husband's lordly anger and those great hairy gorilla hands upon his throat. Challenger did not suffer fools—nor anyone else for that matter—lightly.

Malone grew nervous, his mind recalled those memories with grave concern. He knew he must seek a more nimble approach—however, the Professor would not allow him that way out.

"Malone! You rascal!" The Professor's voice bellowed in a throaty roar as if reading his mind. Now the newsman grew fearful, for he well knew this is how it began with Challenger; working himself up into a frenzy of anger, then rage. The professor was well known for having assaulted various impertinent persons in his career and had been the subject of numerous court cases, so the newsman did not take his volatile anger lightly nor frivolously.

"No, not I, Professor Challenger, I assure you, sir."

"Then get to it, Malone! My time is valuable, you know! Genius waits for no man."

Malone nodded, quickly explaining that his editor had tasked him to write a feature article about what Challenger saw as the scientific causes of the *Titanic* tragedy—if there were any. It was the one-year anniversary of the great disaster.

Challenger seriously considered the premise for a moment, then suddenly boomed in agreement, "I have thought upon that very subject since it first occurred, and have collected evidence that will shed new light upon the disaster. So I accept your request, Malone. When do we get to work?"

"Well, ah, Professor, that is the one caveat, for I will not be working with you this time. Not until I return. Professor Summerlee and Lord John Roxton are also not available."

"What! Well explain yourself, young man!"

"Mr. McArdle is most insistent that I leave at once from Liverpool tomorrow to take ship to New York, where I am to interview the American president. Professor Summerlee is incommunicado, doing research in some corner of darkest Africa, while Lord John is off hunting in the faraway jungles of Siam."

"I see," Challenger blurted unhappily. "So I am to do all the work, spend all my time and energy and then present to you my findings, information I researched so hard to complete? Then you write your article upon your return and take all the credit?"

"Absolutely not! No, it is not like that at all, sir, I assure you, but if you do not mind…"

"Hah! I most certainly do mind! You abuse me, my young friend!" Challenger growled and Malone could see the rage brewing in the older man's beetling brows, his twisted mouth and his blustery manner growing dangerously close to the red zone.

"Of course not, sir! I would never be party to such a thing. Since Summerlee, Lord John and I will not be available, I have arranged a new team to join you in this endeavour."

"A new *team*? I need no "team," Malone, I am my own *team!* I am not asking for any team, simply some competent assistance. I have my research notes all prepared upon this subject and have formulated my theory. Do you think I have not thought upon the roots of this tragedy since the very moment I heard of it?"

"Of course, Professor," the newsman replied demurely, but with all earnestness.

Challenger looked at Malone carefully, showing his imperious and insufferable lordly manner, as his wondrous mind thought over the implications.

"Malone?" Challenger asked his guest in a quiet voice loaded with dangerous suspicion, "by the by, my lad, just for curiosity's sake, if nothing else, who have you engaged?"

Malone thought quickly; this would be a most delicate explanation. "Well, Professor, they are three good men of note."

"I am waiting, Malone!"

The young man swallowed hard, blurted, "You know them, sir, or know *of* them surely; Doctor John H Watson…and the Holmes Brothers."

"Hah! Well, that is just impossible! I mean, this Watson is a medical man and may be of some use, but the others…The Holmes Brothers, you say? I know of Mycroft certainly, a superior mind without doubt, but he will surely never leave the confines of his beloved Diogenes Club, so he is a non-starter, but that younger Holmes brother…?"

"Sherlock."

"Yes, that pompous, arrogant mountebank Sherlock Holmes!" Challenger boomed in rough rage. The young newsman feared the man might turn violent any moment.

Malone spoke quickly, pleadingly, "They are all worthy fellows, Professor, I assure you, and each one has much to offer you in your great work. They are all onboard and agreeable, and only await your assent for them to join you here."

Challenger grunted, then surprisingly shrugged his mighty shoulders, "Well, I can stomach Mycroft Holmes and Doctor Watson well enough, I have heard both are intelligent and scientific men, after all, but this Sherlock Holmes fellow? Why is he interested in this project? I propose to you the man has some ulterior motive for his involvement. In fact, I am certain of it."

"It does not matter, sir, for he is willing, and so are the others, and all three I am sure will be of inestimable help to you."

"Inestimable help? Malone, you are a clod, you arrange this fiasco just as you disembark these shores by steamship on the morrow. You disappoint me, young man. Nevertheless, I am a most magnanimous fellow, as all can surely attest, so with reluctance I will agree to your offer. Very well, you may tell these men to come here tomorrow, then I shall see what their true game is!"

HOLMES AND WATSON ARE DRAWN IN:

"Well, Holmes, I say, you look rather grim this evening. I gather you have heard from Malone?" Doctor Watson asked, noting his friend's intense demeanour.

"Malone and Mycroft," Holmes replied sharply. "This is a dangerous game. Of course, you know my brother has taken himself out of the picture, so you and I are on our own for this one."

"Well, that is certainly not quite cricket of him," Watson said, his feathers a bit ruffled. "I mean, Malone enlisting Mycroft's aid in something or other that he and you will not divulge to me; then Malone sails off across the Pond to New York. Now your brother opts out as well and leaves us holding the bag."

"I know nothing of Malone, but that is Mycroft, for good or ill, I am afraid."

"Well, I don't like it, Holmes. We do not even have any idea why we are to see this Professor Challenger."

"I have some idea, good Watson, and it may be of the utmost importance. Malone has engaged us, ostensibly to help the Professor in some scientific research, something pertaining to the *Titanic* tragedy, but Mycroft has told me of a more pressing issue."

"Ah, so now we get to the nub of the story."

"Indeed, Watson. You are perhaps familiar with the reputation of this Professor George Edward Challenger?"

"Yes, of course. I have heard the stories and they abound. He is said to be a man of incredible intellect and just as incredible temper. He is a brawler."

"More than that, he is a misanthrope, a man not born out of his century—but born out of his millennium," Holmes added.

"It is no secret even his colleagues hate him," Watson responded.

"And with good reason, my friend. Professor Challenger, though a brilliant man, is certainly the most insufferable fellow in all of England. He beats the world for offensiveness. Nevertheless, we must find a way to deal with him."

"Why is that, Holmes?"

"Because there will be an assassination attempt made upon his life in the next day or two and we must prevent it at all costs."

"But surely Mycroft's people, or Scotland Yard, can place guards at his home to forestall any such attempt?"

"Challenger would never accept such an arrangement. He is impossible in that regard as in most others. It is up to you and I to see this through. You are packed and ready to go? Then we leave tomorrow morning at first light, then catch our train at Victoria Station."

THE DETECTIVE AND THE PROFESSOR:

"There it is, Watson, Challenger's house at Enmore Park. It has been a long trip, but we shall be there soon, so steel yourself, for I assure you this man can be most difficult," Holmes warned as the small trap, drawn by a single horse, slowly brought the pair to the front yard of the great man's home. Holmes paid the driver, and Watson gathered their two small valises in hand; then, with heavy hearts, both men walked up the cobble pathway to the front door.

Watson looked at that door with some trepidation, then shot a wary glance to his companion. "Well, here we are, Holmes."

Holmes nodded, telling the doctor, "Go on then, ring the bell and let us begin what I am sure will prove to be a most singular adventure."

Watson took a deep breath and rang the bell. Immediately, the two men heard a loud bellowing voice roaring in answer from the other end of the house, "Go away!"

Watson looked askance at Holmes, but his companion only smiled. "Ring it again, old fellow."

Watson did as Holmes instructed.

"I told you to go away! Do not make me come out there and thrash you! For I surely will! Newsmen, drummers, interfering annoyances—I'll not have you! Now be gone!"

"Holmes, he sounds like a mad man."

"I have often had the occasion to notice, my good Watson, that there is a thin line between genius and madness and I am sure Professor Challenger possesses both qualities in ample measure."

Watson shook his head in despair. Holmes himself now rang the bell, and continued to ring it again and again until they heard loud footsteps rushing upon the wooden floor inside the house advancing towards them. Suddenly the front door was flung open and there in the doorway stood an enraged Professor Challenger; short, squat, a muscular bull with jet black hair and a coal-black beard that jutted out at them like a dagger. His eyes were a piercing grey, his manner was arrogant and threatening, and his gorilla-like hands were balled up into massive fists that appeared ready to strike out at any moment.

In a bellowing Scotch accent he growled, "My lovely, patient Jessie tells me I must restrain me baser impulses to pummel those who would disturb me from my work."

Watson looked upon the man in utter amazement, wondering if he should have brought his revolver.

Holmes allowed a wry grin, and simply offered his hand in greeting, "I am Sherlock Holmes and this is my friend and colleague, Doctor John Watson. Have I the pleasure of addressing Professor George Edward Challenger?"

"You know you do, sonny!" Challenger blurted, then he reluctantly nodded, but he did not shake hands with Holmes. "All right, then, come in. I told Malone I would see you and I always keep my promises, but for the love of God I can not see what either of you men could contribute to my research upon the *Titanic* disaster. In fact, I am almost complete with that work, so I have no need of your help. As if you could offer any!"

"Really?" Holmes asked, carefully diplomatic, knowing full well that he needed to tread lightly with this man as he entered his house. "I am happy to hear that news and would be most eager to view your findings."

"If you could understand them," Challenger growled, looking at the Great Detective carefully. "The world is full of obtuse clods I am forced to contend with!"

Holmes smiled calmly, "I see."

Watson had had enough by then. He stammered in anger, "Well, really, Professor! I am astounded! You present to us a most rude and offensive manner!"

"Easy, my friend," Holmes cautioned the doctor, but it was too late, for Watson was now on fire.

"No, Holmes, I'll not stand by and listen to this bombastic bore speak to you in such an arrogant manner! He is abominable! We come here to help him and this is the treatment we receive! I'll not countenance such behaviour from this bearded popinjay!"

"Popinjay!" Challenger barked in rage. "I'll show you what a popinjay can do!" Suddenly Challenger crouched down into a low attack stance and charged Watson head-on like a wild bull.

Watson was utterly surprised and totally taken aback by the sudden and most ungentlemanly attack, but Sherlock Holmes had expected just such a situation. He deftly lifted an umbrella from the nearby stand, and upending it, used the hook to grasp the Professor's leg and quickly bring him down to the floor before he could reach Watson.

Challenger hit the floor bellowing in anger, fuming and roaring in rage, "I was tricked! That was entirely unfair of you, sir!"

"And I suppose I should have allowed you to pummel poor Watson here," Holmes stated firmly with cold precision and total control. "I think not. He and I are here at your invitation. I am most disappointed in you, Professor, most disappointed. You are one of the most brilliant men in the British Isles, lo, even in the entire world. It is a shame you resort to such barbarous tactics and can not control your anger. It is, I must say, quite disgusting. Come, Watson, let us leave this man and his house immediately."

"George! George, what have you done?" This now from a high-pitched female voice belonging to a slim, petite, bird-like woman who had just run into the room. It was Challenger's wife, Jessie, and she rushed to her fallen husband.

"Are you all right, dear?" Jessie asked the much chastened Professor as she helped her husband to his feet, for Holmes's words had a most intense effect upon him.

"Yes, my love," Challenger said softly, giving his wife a soft kiss upon the cheek. "I am fine, fine I tell you, now you should get back to your sewing and have no further worries on my behalf. This is Doctor Watson and Mr. Sherlock Holmes. Malone enlisted them to help me and…"

"And you lost your temper again, George, did you not?" his wife scolded him firmly.

"Yes, I am afraid I did, my love."

"Then an apology is in order, is it not, George?"

"Yes, of course. I am sorry, my dear," Challenger said softly.

"Not to me, you ninny, but to these two gentlemen," Jessie instructed him.

Challenger smiled broadly at the rebuke, "Just teasing you, my dear. Yes, of course. Please accept my apology, gentlemen. My words were abominable, but I find these days that I am inundated by too many people, all of whom intrude upon my time and my work. Both of which are precious to me."

"As they should be," Holmes stated, his eyes upon those of the professor. "Let us speak no more of it."

Then the Great Detective held out his hand once again and this time Challenger took it and shook it heartily. Then the same was done with Watson.

"Good, now I will leave you gentlemen to your important work," Jessie Challenger told them as she left the room.

Challenger smiled a broad grin through his thatch of great black beard as he watched her walk out of the room. "That little lady is the love of my life, sirs. I have no idea how she can still put up with me after all these years, but she does."

"You are a most lucky man," Watson stated sincerely.

"You are correct, doctor," Challenger said as he lead his two visitors into his large and comfortable study, closing the door behind him and then offering them seats. "Now tell me the real reason why you are here, Mr. Holmes."

"To help you with your research," Holmes replied simply. "Malone said you needed some helpers."

"Hah! That's a crock! I need no helpers—and in any event my research is all but completed. I have come up with a fascinating theory, something so earthshaking that it may be decades—or even a century—before the world will be ready to understand it."

"Indeed," Holmes spoke up very much interested. "I would be delighted to hear of it. I am sure anything you have discovered will set the conventional scientific world upon its head."

Challenger preened a bit at the compliment, "It certainly will, Mr. Holmes, but at this moment I want the truth of your visit here. The real reason."

Holmes nodded, "Very well, Professor. Within the next forty-eight hours an assassination attempt will be made upon your life."

Challenger was silent for a moment with this grim news, then he laughed uproariously. "Bah! Nonsense! I receive death threats all the time. You have to do better than that, young man. Why, I am sure that half of my colleagues would murder me in my very bed if they had the nerve to do so and could guarantee they would get away with the crime. You have to do better than that. I do not believe you."

"Believe what you will, Professor," Holmes stated firmly, "but Watson and I are here to forestall that attempt. I can not tell you from what source it will come or who is directly behind it, but I can tell you it is not a crime born out of passion of any type. It is a professional job."

"Professional, you say?" Challenger asked thoughtfully. It certainly sounded ominous.

"Absolutely," Holmes added. "Professor, I know that a brilliant man such as yourself works upon many research projects simultaneously. One of these may have attracted the attention of a foreign power. Watson and I are here to prevent the murder of the world's greatest scientist—a man who possesses a brilliant mind of the very first order that can not be allowed to be shut down. It would be a tragic loss to the Empire, to humanity itself!"

"Yes, surely it would," Challenger stated in all seriousness. "But how do you know this? Ah, yes, of course, your brother, Mycroft. So what is the plan?"

"Someone will show himself here within the next forty-eight hours. Until that time Watson and I will be honoured to be your guests and endeavour to help you in your *Titanic* project any way we are able."

Challenger nodded, accepting the terms, then a worried look came to his face. "Tell me, Mr. Holmes, is this assassination connected in any way to my research upon the sinking of the *Titanic*?"

Holmes allowed a slim grin. "Most assuredly not."

"I presumed so, nevertheless I am gratified to hear that. It would grieve me severely if that great tragedy and loss of life were the result of anything other than cruel fate—as in some man-made incident."

"I assure you it was not," Holmes confirmed.

Challenger nodded in relief, "Well, gentlemen, Malone organized this meeting, but I fail to see how you can aid me in my scientific research. That research has been all but completed. All it needs now is for Malone to return later this month and write up my findings for publication."

"Then perhaps Watson and I could be of some little help. As men of natural inquisitiveness, we have our own theory of this tragedy but would be most pleased to hear yours. Eh, Watson?"

"Absolutely, Holmes," Watson replied, looking towards the black-haired, bull-like man seated behind his desk. "Professor Challenger, I can not begin to tell you how thrilled I am to make your acquaintance—I have followed your exploits in the scientific journals and your work is unparalleled."

"Naturally,' Challenger asserted boldly, enjoying the prestige the doctor had bestowed upon him. "Then I shall explain to you my findings, so long as you both are capable of understanding them."

Holmes shot Watson a sharp look of restraint, and the two men patiently waited for Challenger to begin his explanation of the great steamship tragedy.

Challenger began in his great booming voice, "Science, sirs, is a living, breathing, turbulent game. The minute one new discovery has been made it becomes obsolete as the world breathlessly awaits the next one to be made. I feel I have jumped ahead—perhaps by decades—in my findings. I have prepared voluminous books of calculations proving my findings beyond any doubt. I will allow you and the doctor to read them first-hand tomorrow morning. As for now, good sirs, it is rather late and Jessie calls us to dinner."

The two guests then dined with Challenger and his delightful wife, Jessie. Both men were rather astounded by this pairing of the larger-than life misanthropic little Hercules with such a petite and bird-like woman. But the love was certainly there for the guests to plainly see. For Jessie doated on her husband as though he were a young precocious boy of twelve years, and for all his terrible ways, Challenger's gruff edges softened to putty at her loving manner.

The foursome enjoyed a fine meal and afterwards Challenger—knowing something of Mr. Holmes's reputation from Doctor Watson's stories in *The Strand*—inveighed upon his guests to recount one of their most famous cases.

The evening concluded with Challenger giving vent to his own opinions on every topic under the sun. Like an angry lord or some Olympian god of old, he railed against the impurity of science and the clods who were his colleagues. Finally it was time for bed and Jessie led Holmes and Watson to an upstairs spare bedroom, for the Professor would not hear of his guests seeking a hostelry in the local village for the night.

Once Holmes and Watson were alone, the two men were able to speak freely out of the range of Challenger's hearing.

"I am much relieved the Professor invited us to stay here to-night, Watson."

"Yes, these accommodations are far superior to those any local village inn could provide," Watson replied, unpacking his small valise.

Holmes smiled indulgently at his friend. "That is not the reason I had in mind. Challenger is in danger, so it is good we are here in his home to stand watch. With that said, I will take the first four hours and you the second four, old fellow. Is that acceptable?"

"Whatever you say, Holmes."

"Good man, now get some sleep. I will wake you in four hours."

Watson went to bed and was soon asleep snoring rhythmically as Sherlock Holmes stood alert guard, in deep thought on what the morrow would bring.

CHALLENGER'S CHALLENGE:

The night passed without incident and Holmes was sure that was only because of Watson's and his own presence in the house. After dressing, the two guests joined Challenger and his wife in a delightful morning meal before getting to work.

"I am something of an amateur astronomer, gentlemen, and enjoy keeping records of the events of the heavens that I observe with my telescope. I keep voluminous notes," Challenger explained, leading Holmes and Watson to his study. There he picked up two heavy foot-thick binders in his large hairy hands. Carrying one massive binder under each arm he then led his guests outside the house to chairs upon the back yard patio, surrounded by a lovely garden and lush bushes.

"My Jessie suggested we get out of my stuffy study and enjoy the morning air out here in the garden, and of course, she is correct. So sit down, gentlemen, and relax," Challenger said as he seated himself in a chair across from his guests and presented Holmes and Watson each with one of the massive binders.

"What is this?" Watson asked in some wonderment.

"My work, doctor, the facts and figures of it all. Read it and it will make all clear to you as the morning sun," Challenger ordered in a blustery roar.

"Why, it must weigh ten pounds!" Watson said in astonishment, taking the massive tome and looking at it with grave misgivings.

"Only a little over eight pounds, I assure you. I despise padding in scientific calculations but it is all there, not one whit more, nor one whit less," Challenger stated proudly.

"And what are we to do with this, Professor?" Holmes asked calmly.

"Do? Why read it, of course, sir! Read it and learn the brilliance of my discovery!"

Holmes allowed a grimace as he leafed through the massive compilation. Challenger noted the gesture and grew a bit piqued, but Holmes quickly worked to tamp down the man's rising mood, "Professor, there is no doubt your brilliant discovery here is an important one and will offer new information on the *Titanic* tragedy, but poor Watson and I are not scientists, and certainly we do not possess minds that are in your intellectual league."

"That is true, of course," Challenger allowed, staring suspiciously at the two men, "but you should not deride yourselves for your lack of intellect."

Holmes nodded with a tiny smile.

Watson looked imploringly at his detective friend, then to Challenger, "You expect us to read all this? Now, at this moment? Why, it must run to a thousand pages!"

"Eleven-hundred and fifty-five, to be precise," Challenger boomed, "but I kept it purposely…slim. Only the essential information. Now read! Read it all! I will not comment one iota upon my discovery until you have read it all!"

Watson gulped, opened the binder and flipped through the pages. They were for the most part covered with the most obtuse and complicated mathematical calculations. Even Watson, an educated and scientific medical man, could barely make head nor tail of them. He looked imploringly at Holmes for some aid.

Sherlock Holmes simply smiled, opened his book and began reading. Watson shook his head, giving up on any assistance from his friend and tried to get through the first page introductory preface. He soon found himself totally at sea. Astronomy and solar calculations were not his strong point; he only wondered why Holmes was going through with this charade.

"Delve into it, Watson," Holmes boasted in good humour, "it makes for fascinating reading. The Professor has come up with a theory that I feel will rock the very foundations of our conventional knowledge about the *Titanic* disaster."

"Really, Holmes?" Watson asked somewhat dubiously.

"Absolutely, my good man. It is all there plainly written in black and white."

"That it is, Mr. Holmes," Challenger allowed, now in far better humour that his work was being accepted and even praised. "I am gratified to find you appreciating my discovery."

"I am enjoying it immensely," Holmes stated in all seriousness as he turned the page and began reading anew. Watson noted his friend was already a few pages ahead of him into his tome, while he was still struggling through page one of his own mammoth volume.

Challenger sat facing the two men in his chair like a statue, unmoving, his eyes firmly fixed upon the two men before him.

Every once in a while Holmes would look up, look over at the Professor, then look around the house and yard as if digesting the data. Watson merely rubbed his eyes and yearned for the straight-ahead simplicity of the articles in the *Lancet*.

"It does bring thoughtfulness to the mind, does it not, Mr. Holmes?" Challenger asked with obvious delight.

"Indeed it does, Professor. Like all great writing it must be taken in small doses, and digested properly, so its full impact can be properly appreciated."

Challenger beamed, someone actually understood his work! The Professor sat back in his chair with a broad smile breaking through the darkness of his great black beard.

Of course Holmes had noticed the man lurking in the bushes. He had been watching him, and the knife he held intently, for the last few minutes—but he waited. Suddenly the intruder sprang from the bushes and ran towards the Professor. The man—certainly the assassin—held a knife, but Sherlock Holmes had his own weapon. The Great Detective allowed one immeasurable second to pass as the assassin drew closer to his target—then he acted. It all happened so fast Watson barely noticed a thing, and Challenger—whose back was towards the assassin—had absolutely no warning at all.

Once the intruder was within range and behind the Professor, ready to plunge his knife into the great man's back, Holmes immediately flung the heavy book he had been reading in a mighty upward arc which came down precisely upon the assassin's head with a resounding blow. It was like being hit with a cinder block, and the assassin went down to the ground unconscious and bloody.

"Holmes!" Watson shouted in shock.

"My God! What has happened?" Challenger growled. "Not another annoying newshound?"

"Not a newshound, Professor, but your assassin," Holmes stated as he went over to examine the unconscious man. The weighty book had hit the intruder squarely in the head; he would be out for some time. "Watson, please be so kind as to ask the Professor's wife to phone the police."

"Of course, Holmes." Watson set off on his errand.

"Holmes?" Challenger asked, noticing the knife on the ground near the man's hand, which the Great Detective now picked up and examined. "I admit, I did not believe you. Now I must. How did you spot him?"

"This lovely patio garden makes a perfect location for a murder. All these bushes that surround the house offer any attacker plenty of camouflage. Of course I noticed the fellow lurking there immediately we came out here, but I knew you would require proof that there was serious danger. That is why I was so agreeable on Watson and I reading your books. That gave me time to keep track of the man and for him to launch his attack. In the end, if nothing else, your book made a most effective weapon."

"Aye, it just proves all that research does have its uses, eh, Mr. Holmes?" Challenger's voice enthused with joy rather than insult at the remark. "But who is he and why the attack upon my person?"

"If I am not very much mistaken he is a Serbian national, but we may find there are German masters behind him. You are working on some problems for the Admiralty on a new underwater vessel—a submersible, are you not?"

"Why yes, but that is secret. Top secret," Challenger stated guardedly.

"My brother informed me about it. The German navy is likewise working upon such a vessel, what they call a U-boat."

"Ah, yes, the *unterseeboot*. So they seek to put a stop to my work?"

"Precisely," Holmes stated as he bound the still unconscious assassin so that he presented a neat package ready for the police. "Now perhaps you will allow the police protection that Malone and my brother have insisted upon?"

"Aye, Mr. Holmes, G.E.C. will most certainly allow it now."

Watson and Jessie Challenger ran out of the house, Jessie to embrace her husband in tears of joy and relief, the doctor to Holmes. "I called Lestrade, and he will be here soon to take the assassin away. I am sure the man will have much explaining to do."

THE PROFESSOR'S FINDING:

It was now late afternoon and all the excitement of the morning was over. The assassin had been taken away by Scotland Yard and the Challenger home at Enmore Park was once again back to normal.

"You still have not finished reading my findings, Mr. Holmes, Doctor Watson," Challenger asked in a most insistent tone. "Before you leave for London you should experience all that my research has established."

Watson gave an audible moan and looked pleadingly at his friend, whispering, "Please, Holmes, don't let him make me read that entire thing."

Sherlock Holmes smiled at the doctor and looked meaningfully at Professor Challenger, "I suggest a synopsis of your findings might be best, straight from your own lips. That would be far more effective and put this entire matter into perspective far better than any mere text ever could."

"You do not want to read the entire book?" Challenger asked, somewhat chastened.

"Well, actually no, Professor. In any event, poor Watson here would not understand it, and speaking for myself, my own abilities in astronomy and among the higher mathematics is severely limited. I am, after all, no Professor Moriarty."

"Hah! That fraud!" Challenger boomed in anger.

"Nevertheless, a brilliant man, and his treatise upon the binomial theorem …"

"Which he stole from me!" Challenger barked, now flaring rage. "Just as he stole my notes for his much vaunted book, *The Dynamics of an Asteroid!*"

"Most interesting, I had no idea. Well, in any event he is long gone now," Holmes added soothingly.

"And good riddance!"

"So what shall it be, Professor? A brief explanation? Watson and I would be most grateful to hear it."

Challenger nodded, "So be it. Well, where to begin? The *Titanic* tragedy, the sinking of that magnificent ship after hitting an iceberg, the tremendous loss of life…Underlying reasons, sir, that is what I was seeking to discover since first I heard news of the great disaster. The more I thought about the tragedy, the more I could not believe such a thing possible. I tell you it galled me massively. Surely nothing so devastating had ever happened before in maritime history? So then, there had to be some reason behind it, and that reason must be exceptional. Then I came upon something extraordinary."

Challenger stopped his narration, looking off into the sky as if he could see and hear the disaster taking place before him.

"Please continue, Professor," Holmes prompted.

"What I found," Challenger stated, as if giving a lecture to two of his students, "was that climatic conditions were overall responsible for what had occurred. Specifically, exceptionally strong tides allowed the iceberg field to form, and which struck the *Titanic*. Now icebergs have been known to be a menace in those North Atlantic waters for decades by seamen. The captain of the ship even set his course in a more southerly direction to avoid them. However, my research shows a convergence of three astronomical events which exaggerated the effects of tidal forces upon the Atlantic Ocean." Challenger took a deep breath, then continued. "It was a unique combination of these three astronomical events. The Moon was full on January 4, which created what we call a spring tide. That means the tide-raising forces combine to greater net effect. At the same time the Moon was at perigee—at its closest point to the Earth. This caused an eccentric orbit that enhanced the gravitational pull on our planet. The Earth was also at perihelion—its closest point to the Sun. This boosts the Sun's gravitational influence."

"I fail to see…" Watson blurted impatiently.

"Bear with me, doctor," Challenger demanded in a surprisingly patient tone. "It was all due to the increased tidal force created on January 4 and the perigees of December 6 and February 2—these effects raised the sea level and that refloated hundreds of icebergs that had been held fast in the low waters off the Greenland coast. Some of them held for many years, in fact. Because of these events and the higher than normal tides, these icebergs broke free to float south, eventually to doom the unlucky ship. The *Titanic* blindly cruised under the pitch blackness of a dark moon that fateful night straight into a field of hundreds, if not thousands, of deadly iceberg traps. I am afraid there could have been no other result."

"Amazing, Professor!" Watson cried, then he added sadly, "So the poor ship had no chance?"

Sherlock Holmes nodded gravely. "No chance at all. It is a powerful theory, Professor."

"Aye, powerful, Mr. Holmes, but no one will believe it, I am afraid. Leastways not today, nor tomorrow, but perhaps some day they will."

"Some day," Holmes stated, "we will possess the science to prove your calculations, then history shall record that it was the power of the Moon and tides that set into motion events that sank the ship that was called unsinkable—R.M.S. *Titanic*. You have done exceptional work, sir."

Challenger beamed, "As have you and Doctor Watson. I thank you both most gratefully. You stopped an assassination attempt that surely, if successful, would have severely interfered with my work—and no doubt caused my dearest Jessie undue distress."

"I am sure such an event would upset her most severely," Holmes added with a slim smile, then added, "Professor, it has been a pleasure to make your acquaintance and to learn the truth behind the *Titanic* tragedy."

"Not bad for an honest days work, eh, Mr. Holmes? Just wait until Malone hears of this!"

HISTORICAL NOTE:

Much research has been done into the sinking of R.M.S. *Titanic*. Books abound and theories do as well. Many are interesting but inconclusive. Challenger's findings presented by him in this story set in 1913 had to wait almost a hundred years before being verified by science. In 1995, Fergus Wood suggested the Moon's perigee of January 4, 1912, may have had a role in the sinking of the great ship by freeing up the icebergs from the Jakobshaun Glacier in Greenland. Further research was more recently done by Don Olson, Russell Doescher and Roger Sinnott for their article in *Sky & Telescope* magazine's April 2012 issue entitled, "Did The Moon Sink The Titanic?" It offers a fascinating and very plausible theory on just what might have happened to allow the deadly iceberg to meet the ill-fated luxury liner. The rest, as they say, is history.

WE HATE THE TASTE OF JELLYFISH

by Jay Carey

The sea was white with jellyballs, and the tide was leaving them by the thousands on Sarasota's submerged Bayfront Drive, where it was easy to pick them up. Everyone was carrying buckets or cooking pots to carry them in. It was 2048, and sometimes it seemed that the rapidly acidifying ocean was turning into a soup of jellyfish.

A mother and daughter, Silvia and Pilar Nunez, were working not far from an abandoned bus shelter, where they had already placed a couple of full pails on a bench. Both women were ankle-deep in water, scooping up the white, mushroom-shaped creatures with nets. They had to make sure there was enough water in the containers to keep the jellyfish alive until they could be dried properly. At the same time, Silvia was fretting because she thought a wave might swamp her bucket and carry the jellyfish away. Both women were wearing awkward-looking rubber boots. Jellyballs were not particularly poisonous, as jellyfish went, but no sane person liked to be stung.

The women were discussing Pilar's romantic prospects. Or rather, Silvia was fretting about those, too, and Pilar was fending her off as best she could. She was embarrassed that her mother was speaking so freely in public. Silvia indiscreetly described one of the suitors as a loser and the other, who owned the restaurant where Pilar worked, as well-fixed and maybe not as dull as he appeared.

There were a dozen people catching jellyfish on this stretch of highway at the time, and any one of them could have known the two men personally. In fact, an old woman in a long purple-flowered skirt straightened up and said to Pilar, "You won't have the choice for long."

As Silvia said later to Detective Eureka Kilburn, the woman was holding her skirt up out of the water higher than she needed to, considering her age. Her lips were bright red, and her eyelids were violet. What footwear she had on you couldn't tell, but it certainly wasn't anything like boots. She was holding only one container, a large black pot.

Mother and daughter simply stared, not wishing to encourage her.

"Prosper Jean will be dead by Saturday," the old woman elaborated.

The restaurant owner courting Pilar was indeed named Prosper Jean. His establishment, the Fire Pit, was the most popular in town. He'd started out delivering wild hog he'd hunted, butchered, and grilled himself. Then, as eating places all over Florida were shutting down, he took one over, adding to its menu a stew of potatoes, tomatoes, and spiced nutria that Eureka still marveled at. It was so tasty no one minded on the days there wasn't any boar, which was just as well, as those days were becoming increasingly frequent.

Lots of people knew that Prosper Jean had been courting his waitress, Pilar Nunez. More surprising was that he did die by Saturday—on Saturday, in fact.

"It was amazing," said Silvia down at the police station on the day of the funeral. She didn't sound amazed, though. She sounded angry. Prosper was only thirty years old, she said, vigorous and healthy. It was true that he was on the heavy side, but he was bulky rather than fat. There was no reason he should have died.

Silvia Nunez had aged a lot in the past decade. Detective Eureka Kilburn remembered her younger face so clearly that the odd triangular lines above her eyebrows and the deep wrinkles at the corners of her mouth looked as if they'd been drawn on by an inexpert make-up artist. Eureka wondered what exactly had brought her down to the station. "What bothers you?" she asked. "The death? Or the prediction?"

"The doctor put heart failure as the cause of death."

Det. Kilburn nodded. Dr. Fogarty had told her that the heart had stopped beating for no discernible reason. It couldn't have been a heart attack of any type. Kidneys, lungs, liver were all fine. The tox screen showed nothing. Up north that might have been a red flag. Down here, it was assumed that living in Florida had killed him. Prosper Jean's restaurant was a success, and his situation seemed to be a salutary one, considering—but the stuff you had to consider these days was pretty bad: hotter and hotter days, constant flooding, swarms of jellyfish, etc., etc.

"Do you think anyone can really foretell the future?" said Silvia.

"Offhand I would say it was a lucky guess. Of course she may have been a health professional." Although Eureka had an idea of who the old woman might have been, and she did not qualify.

"You think so?"

"Well, no." The detective frowned. Coincidences happened all the time—crazier coincidences than that. But still…. "It's hard even for professionals to guess the exact day someone is going to die."

"It's spooky."

These words were so perfunctory Det. Kilburn knew that the reason for the visit was not skittishness over a possible occult event. "I can't do anything about that," she said with a smile.

"There was a fierce rivalry for my daughter between Prosper Jean and another man," said Silvia, finally getting to the point. "And I have heard of untraceable poisons…"

"It's not they are really untraceable. It's that the traces disappear by the time anyone looks for them. Or maybe we can't afford the test."

Silvia ignored her. "My daughter may be worried that her surviving admirer was involved in the other's death. Prosper fired him just a few days before he died, and he was really angry."

She looked at Det. Kilburn significantly.

"I see," said Eureka. "And who is the young man causing all this worry?" She did not point out that it seemed to be the mother who was doing the worrying.

His name was Sami Roy, and Silvia was not a fan. He was in his mid-twenties. He used to do odd jobs at the restaurant, and even after he was fired he hung around trying to talk to Pilar. He had soulful black eyes and a full sensuous mouth that young girls were taken in by. Some people said the longish black hair that waved away from his face was like a picture of Jesus. Silvia considered this blasphemy. Sami's character was an example to no one. He spent most of his time daydreaming and the rest of it drinking. He was not a serious person.

"And now it turns out he might be capable of violence," she added. "My daughter is my life. I'm afraid the shock of Prosper's death will drive her into his arms. Maybe you could stop by the funeral and check things out?"

Det. Kilburn asked Silvia to look at some pictures first. It took her only a few minutes to create a photo line-up around a woman named Mizwillah, who'd recently opened a shop called The Third Eye. Eureka marveled at the images in the line-up as she turned the screen toward Silvia. How wonderful it would be if the electricity were always up and running like this.

Silvia immediately identified Mizwillah as the old woman in the purple-flowered skirt, then said nervously, "I'll go on ahead. I have to meet my daughter before the funeral. There's no reason to tell her I've stopped by, is there?"

"Not yet," said Det. Kilburn, turning in her swivel chair, a piece of furniture confiscated from a nearby real estate office—now defunct, as most of the houses in Sarasota had been abandoned. "You know the Third Eye?"

"I've seen the sign," said Silvia. "Sami goes there. You think that's where he could have gotten the poison?" She seemed to take it for granted that the young man would be acquainted with someone whose photo was found in the police files.

"Let's not get ahead of ourselves."

Silvia Nunez was a hard-headed widow. Det. Kilburn knew Pilar less well, but she was beautiful and apparently amiable. Even in this day and age, such a combination could be parlayed into a certain amount of comfort for a young lady and her justifiably frightened mother. Although jellyballs filled you up, their texture was unpleasant, and they generally tasted like the vinegar they were preserved in.

It was no wonder that Silvia was angry about Prosper Jean's sudden and inexplicable death. But she may have been in too much of a hurry to pick out a person to blame. Was it because she wanted to protect her daughter from a violent man? Or from a poor one?

The funeral was held at St. Dominic's on Fruitville Rd. Det. Kilburn left an hour to get there because she did not see how she could justify using up any of the squad car's gas. On her walk she noted the sign for The Third Eye. In addition to fortune telling, Mizwillah sold various love spells and other, darker potions. When Eureka dropped by a couple of days before, Mizwillah repaid the favor by telling her she would soon meet with professional success.

Det. Kilburn had changed from her uniform to some lightweight black slacks for the funeral. She liked and admired Mizwillah's manner of dress but couldn't have stood it for herself. Her slacks were reminiscent of the plain trim khakis of the police uniform. They were exotic in a way different from Mizwillah's wardrobe. They were exotic in their neatness, a rarity when there was no longer enough electricity to run washing machines and dryers. Eureka walked slowly in order to preserve their crispness for as long as possible. Still she arrived with plenty of time to take a place at the back of the congregation and keep a close watch on everyone who walked in.

A sister church in Harrisburg, Pennsylvania, provided scant resources to help keep up the physical structure, but any kind of maintenance was more than what most buildings in Florida got now. Some of the stained glass windows remained, and the Stations of the Cross were looking pretty good.

The pews were filling up fast, which may have had something to do with the prospect of a gathering at the restaurant afterward. Det. Kilburn recognized Pilar with her mother, who pretended not to see her. Sami Roy was easy to pick out. He was the very attractive dark-haired young man who kept looking over at Pilar. He sat down with his mother and little brother a few pews in front of Eureka. It didn't seem to have occurred to anyone but Silvia to blame him for Prosper's death. People nodded to him and his family, and no one seemed to avoid sitting in the seats around them. Mizwillah arrived after the mass began.

Eulogies had not been allowed by the Catholic Church until recently, and here the innovation was enthusiastically embraced. Mainly the speeches were about the speakers themselves: how they felt about Prosper Jean, what Prosper Jean had done for them, and some important stuff that had happened to them as a result. All the customers considered themselves to be his special friend. They referred to his wry jokes and his melancholy.

Then Pilar Nunez rose. She looked especially small and slender in the expanse of the church, but she spoke with clarity and force. Her face was narrow, and her voice was thin and high and sweet.

She read her speech from a piece of paper. She did not look up often, but when she did, you could sense her bewilderment.

"I owe so much to Prosper," she began. "He was an unfailingly kind and attentive man. I never did thank him properly. I tried to recently, and he didn't believe me.

"When he hired me as a waitress it was because I needed a job, not because he had a position to fill. I didn't realize this until later. He never told me so himself.

"Living in Florida has its challenges, as we all know. But it's where my mother grew up. Where I grew up. It's our home. Prosper knew what it was like to love such a difficult place. I was so young when I started working at the restaurant that I used to babble all sorts of childish hopes and fears and confusions. He listened to me as seriously as he listened to the president of the bank."

Here she looked up. "Remember when there was still a bank in town?" The question held a wistful humor that elicited a few smiles.

"Of course his restaurant was a big success," she said. "Deservedly so. No will ever forget his deep-froth cocoa."

More smiles.

"But he never got so comfortable that he didn't understand what it was like to be lost."

She looked off through the oak-framed glass doors in back of the congregation. "I'm not sure I have the right to speak. I took more than I gave. Sometimes you don't speak soon enough, and sometimes you speak too soon. I don't know which I regret more.

"I hope that somewhere he is forgiving me now. And I hope you can hear me, Prosper, thanking you. Out loud. As I will for the rest of my life."

She struck Eureka as a good-hearted young woman, anxious and concerned, but not someone in despair.

Sami Roy got up next. You might say he bounded up. He did not have notes. He faced the congregation and said, "I wasn't going to speak. But...now I have to. Prosper had some set ideas of how you were supposed to behave, and I know I didn't always conform to them. I should have. It's as simple as that. He was right to fire me. He always treated me fairly, and I repaid him with irresponsibility and tardiness. It was hard on me at the time, but I learned an important lesson from him. I'm grateful, I really am."

He sounded relieved and happy, almost too much so, really, for a funeral.

After a few more customers spoke, and after a long pause to make sure everyone else had finished, the old woman known as Mizwillah moved to the front. She was wearing a floor-length black sheath dress and kitten heels, her lips were dark red, and there were sparkles on her forehead.

Det. Kilburn had met her shortly after moving to Sarasota. Mizwillah was in the police files because she started out as a prostitute. She used a number of different names, including some oddities like Mula. By the time Eureka joined the force, she was running a brothel, having settled on the name Miss Willa. You wouldn't think she could get too old for this sort of managerial position, but gradually, over the years, she left one of her young ladies in charge, and she eventually opened the Third Eye under the name Mizwillah.

From the lectern on the side of the altar, she said, "Death is terrifying. If anyone wants to talk to me about it, I welcome them." Then she retook her seat.

The church seemed to have sponsored its competition. Maybe there was a good reason eulogies had been banned for all those years.

On the other hand, now that Eureka had heard them, she had a good idea of how Prosper Jean had met his end.

As the congregants stood and started to file out—with unusual speed, it seemed, thanks to the prospective meal at the Fire Pit—Sami Roy turned around, his face sunny. Det. Kilburn strode quickly down the outside aisle, brushing by a few startled teenagers. Then she slid into the pew beside him and complimented him on his speech as his mother and brother moved on. She was counting on the setting to induce a relaxed yet truthful conversation.

Sami said, "Oh, the poor guy."

Eureka did not trust his sympathy. It sounded a lot like he was propping himself up with it. But he was happy, there was no mistaking that. She did not believe he was burdened by guilt of any kind. Pilar, on the other hand...

Det. Kilburn noticed her cutting slowly across the crowd in the center aisle toward her young man friend. Behind her was Silvia, torn. She wanted to come over as well to monitor what was happening. But finally her desire to avoid Det. Kilburn—and maybe Sami—prevailed. She busied herself talking to an acquaintance on the other side of the church.

Pilar joined Sami warily, giving Det. Kilburn a questioning glance. Eureka didn't know either of them, really, and that probably meant they were good kids. But Pilar was definitely worried.

"Your speeches were the most heartfelt," Eureka said, which they seemed to appreciate.

Prosper Jean had apparently possessed no family, no old girlfriend, no boyhood buddy. Everyone was a business acquaintance, including Pilar and Sami, but the two of them had veered into more.

"I'm not necessarily looking for an explanation of Mr. Jean's death," said Eureka, "but if I were, I'd do well to have listened closely to what the two of you were saying. Your words contained all sorts of undercurrents of meaning."

"Like what?" said Pilar, trying to hide her alarm.

"Let's see," said Det. Kilburn. "First off, your heart is not broken, or you wouldn't have made the lighthearted references that you did, about the bank and the cocoa."

"I was very fond of him," Pilar protested. "Prosper himself often made jokes about sad things."

"Yes," said Eureka. "You were comfortable speaking that way because you knew him so well. But the other speeches lead me to believe that Mr. Jean's humor was often full of anguish. Is that right?"

"I suppose so."

"Your tone, on the other hand, was more…jittery."

Det. Kilburn paused to think about how best to express her next point. In her eulogy Pilar had dwelled on how she hadn't thanked Prosper Jean properly. Presumably that's what she meant when she said she hadn't spoken soon enough about something. But what did she regret speaking too soon about? She was deeply bothered by it, whatever it was. The most obvious possibility was that she'd told him she had no romantic interest in him. She wouldn't have wanted her decision to be general knowledge because she didn't want her mother to hear. But she thought he should know.

"You feel bad because you couldn't return his feelings for you. And you're sorry you told him when you did because his heart was about to give out, anyway, right? So why did he have to know? Why did you have to spoil his last few days?"

"Yeah," said Pilar. "That's about it. I guess you can read me all right. He would get so sad sometimes. He told me once last year that he was running from a hole that was going to swallow him up. Maybe it did."

It sounded like she'd been reading a few undercurrents of meaning herself. "You were a good friend to him," Eureka told her.

"I wasn't," said Sami Roy.

"And I've never seen anyone so inappropriately happy about that fact at a funeral," said Det. Kilburn. "But you must have just learned from Ms. Nunez's speech that she harbored no deep feelings for Mr. Jean, right?"

Sami nodded, somewhat dazed.

"That's why you were so gleeful about accepting your guilt. Maybe you figured that's why you were fired. Even better, you figured you'd won Ms. Nunez here."

"Well, at least he hasn't lost me," said Pilar.

Eureka smiled. "It's up to the two of you to figure that out."

And it was up to Eureka to deal with Mizwillah. The trials of young lovers everywhere were all very well, but what had interested Det. Kilburn the most about this problem from the beginning was that uncanny prediction. She still could not explain it satisfactorily.

Eureka was more than thirty years younger than Mizwillah. There were striking differences between them, yet there were similarities as well. Eureka admired her independence and resilience. That is probably why she hadn't mentioned to Silvia the most logical explanation for Mizwillah's prediction: She knew when Prosper Jean was going to die because she was going to kill him herself.

Det. Kilburn searched the crowd with her eyes. These were hardworking people for the most part. But it took a rare combination of shrewdness, luck, and sheer stubbornness to survive in Florida during such uncertain times. The rest of the country could no longer send down the aid they used to after a hurricane hit. Det. Kilburn, the Nunezes, the Roys, Mizwillah were on their own. If Silvia Nunez was desperate enough to hustle her daughter, maybe

Mizwillah had been trying to engineer some dramatic proof of her new fortune-telling services.

The main problem with this theory was its silliness. Eureka could see Mizwillah killing out of passion or even—in certain circumstances—for direct financial gain. But to fulfill her prophecy? It would not necessarily benefit her. There were too many variables.

Det. Kilburn spotted her down on the broken-up concrete in front of the church. She'd attracted a number of the curious, including two relatives of the seriously ill.

"I heard about your prediction," said Det. Kilburn, as everybody on the stairs parted for her.

"Many people did," said Mizwillah with satisfaction.

"I'd like to talk to you about it."

Mizwillah nodded, and the two of them fell into step together, heading for the Fire Pit. "There is no subject that interests me more than death," she said.

"I can see why," said Det. Kilburn. "You must have given Prosper Jean the medicine he used. There's no other reason you'd have such an intimate knowledge of his intentions." Suicide was credible more because of his depressive personality than because of the bad news he'd received from Pilar Nunez, but Det. Kilburn supposed they were related. She saw no need to advertise either possibility, however.

"Prosper did come by the shop," said Mizwillah.

She would not have interfered with his plans. She had always argued that victimless crimes should not be called crimes at all. She claimed that people should be able to do anything they liked as long as they didn't hurt anyone else.

"He'd have been better off with a more experienced woman," she confided.

"I'm sure you're right," said Det. Kilburn. "But how did you know when he was going to take the stuff?"

"When I gave it to him, I told him it had a shelf life of four days."

Ah, yes. Mizwillah might not be capable of killing to prove her prophetic powers, but she'd certainly be capable of something subtler—lying to a suicidal man about the properties of a poison. It was easier to predict the future when you're making it yourself.

THE DISAPPEARANCE OF THE VATICAN EMISSARY

by Jack Grochot

During my association with the case work of my friend Sherlock Holmes, no other investigation rendered more depravity or more contradiction than the disappearance of Cardinal Giovanni Tosca. The role Holmes played in the drama was a credit to his ingenuity and tenacity as well as to his brilliant powers of deduction.

We were seated in the armchairs of our Baker Street apartment, I reading an account in *The Times* of the Cardinal vanishing in the nighttime, while Holmes was preoccupied with notes he was making in preparation for writing an article on the advantages of the microscope in the art of detection.

"Organized religion," he blurted, as if knowing my thoughts, "seems more concerned with the process than with the actual worship of the Almighty."

"Indeed!" said I, noting that since the time we met two years earlier in the hospital laboratory, the subject of the spiritual had never once come up, until now. I wondered aloud how he had drifted from concentration on the microscope to matters involving a Supreme Being.

"I couldn't help but notice you were absorbed in the column detailing the disappearance of the Cardinal," said Holmes, "and I couldn't resist the comment to test your sentiment on the topic. We must take care not to allow our attitude to affect the relationship with our visitor this morning." Without waiting for a response, Holmes half stood and reached onto the acid-stained deal-topped table for a letter that had been delivered while I was out for a morning walk around the neighbourhood. He tossed it over to me, and it landed on top of the newspaper that I had set down upon my knees when our conversation had begun.

"Perhaps, my dear Watson," said Holmes cryptically, "this missive will contribute to the suspense of the Cardinal's predicament."

This is what I read:

> Villa Bella Roma
> April 15, 1884
> My Brother in Christ, Mr Sherlock Holmes:
> As secretary to Cardinal Tosca, I implore you to set aside your current activities to exclusively take up the cause of finding His Eminence. Since reports in the public press are sketchy at best, I shall visit your quarters at eleven o'clock to provide whatever additional facts your inquiry would require. In the meantime, both he and you will remain in my prayers.
> Yours faithfully,
> Monsignor Ramo Rossi

"It is most unusual," said I, "that the Monsignor would appeal to you when he already has reported the matter to the official police force. According to *The Times*, not just one detective but a team of detectives has been working to locate Cardinal Tosca."

"Results," said Sherlock Holmes. "It is results, Watson, that are lacking. I am the court of last resort, and Monsignor Rossi is expecting me to succeed where the official police have failed."

It was nearly eleven o'clock already. I had barely enough time to consult Holmes's index on the bookshelf before the Monsignor arrived.

"See what we have on the Cardinal," Holmes had urged, "if anything at all. He appears to be an enigmatic figure, owing to his assignment as a papal emissary, or so *The Times* intimates."

Nonetheless, there was an entry under T.

"Tosca, Giovanni, Cardinal," it stated. "Born in Venice, ordained in Rome, elevated to Bishop of Palermo, consecrated Cardinal in 1875, personal representative of Pope Leo XIII."

"A bare-bones portrait, is it not?" Holmes asked rhetorically as he put aside his notes and replaced the volume in its proper order. "Possibly the Monsignor will oblige us with a more complete biography of the Cardinal. It's always useful to know as much as one can about a missing person. One never knows where it will lead. I remember the little problem of the missing financier, Jacob Nestor, whose family and the police suspected had been abducted and murdered by a rival's henchmen. If only they had learned that he secretly kept a wife and daughter in Australia, the puzzle would have been solved before I was consulted. As it so happened, I was forced to expose his secret and cause Nestor to surface here in order to save two men from the gallows for killing him.

"Well, Watson, here comes our opportunity to learn more about Cardinal Tosca," Holmes concluded as he was interrupted by a ring at the bell.

The sound of his rapid footfall on the stairs indicated a young man. Mrs Hudson, our landlady, had been apprised by Holmes to expect the Monsignor, and so no introduction by her was necessary.

"Come in, Monsignor," Holmes invited as he opened the door before the priest could knock. "This is my colleague and confidant, Dr Watson, before whom you may say anything which you would say to me alone."

Holmes motioned toward the basket-chair as he and I took up positions again in the armchairs, facing Monsignor Rossi.

The light from our two broad windows bathed his features. Young, as we had presumed, the cleric bore a striking resemblance to the handsome stage actor Sir Godfrey Chambliss, whose stern square jaw, black wavy hair combed straight back, and deep-set eyes were a trademark, as was his youthful vigour. Monsignor Rossi spoke perfect English, but with a distinct Italian accent.

"I come here today on behalf of His Holiness, the Pope," said he. "It is he who wishes to engage your services, Mr Holmes, in the interest of locating Cardinal Tosca before any harm comes to him."

"I can assure you," said Holmes, "that I have cleared my calendar to assist in whatever manner I am able. Pray tell, what is the Cardinal's mission in London?"

"My, but you do get right to the point, Mr Holmes," replied Monsignor Rossi. "His mission is very confidential. Were it to be revealed publicly, a scandal would result, no doubt. But I have been authorized to tell you, only if you were to ask, because we believe it may have some bearing on the disposition of this case. What I mean to say is that it could lead you to the Cardinal's whereabouts."

"Your secret is safe with us," Holmes assured.

The Monsignor continued:

"The Cardinal had an appointment with a powerful and influential member of the Italian community, Mario Sacco, whose recent injudicious conduct has come to the attention of His Holiness. Mr Sacco, you see, has divided his loyalties between the Pope and the Archbishop of Canterbury. Mr Sacco began a few months ago to generously give financial support to the Church of England as well as to the Roman Catholic Church, the true church of our Lord, Jesus Christ.

"Mr Sacco does this under the apprehension that he can expand his power and influence to include many more Protestants of London, among whom he wishes to do a great deal of business.

"Cardinal Tosca was commissioned to dissuade Mr Sacco from making a mistake that would ensure his eternal damnation. His Eminence was given permission by the Holy Father himself to warn Mr Sacco that continued support of the Church of England would result in his excommunication from the Catholic fold.

"The appointment with Mr Sacco took place Tuesday afternoon, and it was Tuesday night that the Cardinal was last seen."

"Last seen by whom?" Holmes wanted to know.

"By the coachman for Ambassador Panzini, Ambassador Arturo Panzini, who represents Italy in its dealings with the United Kingdom. His Eminence and I were staying together at the home of Ambassador Panzini. It was I who went to the Cardinal's room on Wednesday morning and found that his bed was never slept in. As was his custom, he had gone among the servants for night prayers on Tuesday, and in the apartment above the stables he convinced the coachman to take him somewhere after they said the rosary together."

"To take him where?"

"This is the inexplicable part of the story, Mr Holmes. His Eminence asked the coachman to take him to Upper Swandam Lane, a vile alley on the north side of the river to the east of London Bridge."

"Curious, very curious," said Holmes. "What business could Cardinal Tosca have had there?" he asked, putting his fingertips together and closing his eyelids.

"None, none whatsoever," answered the Monsignor. "After all, I, his consort, would know if he had any purpose in going there. In any event, the coachman did as requested after hitching up his team to the Ambassador's brougham at almost midnight."

"It defies explanation, but we have so few facts upon which to base a theory," said Holmes. "It may be that after an interview with the Ambassador and the coachman we may know enough to make some suppositions."

"Scotland Yard already has talked with them," informed the Monsignor, "and is no clearer on the matter than in the beginning. Four of Scotland Yard's best men have been put on the case because of the importance of the Cardinal. Inspector Lestrade is in charge. His Holiness wishes for you to assist him."

"Ah, Lestrade," Holmes moaned. "He is one of their best men, to be sure, but my hopes of their bringing the case to a successful conclusion are no brighter because of it. Did he ask you for a biography of the Cardinal? I assumed not. Do your best to write one up for me, then."

Holmes promised to visit the residence of the Ambassador in the next few hours, and he escorted the Monsignor down the stairs and to the front door, where a hansom awaited him. When Holmes returned to the sitting-room he was pensive.

"Well, Watson, what do you make of it?" he asked without first offering an opinion.

"I can make nothing of it, except that the Cardinal has placed himself in jeopardy," came my exasperated reply.

"I fear the worst for Cardinal Tosca," said he. "This man Sacco is more than a common businessman. He is the head of a criminal enterprise, the patriarch of a violent family that deals in prostitution and usury. He is connected to the Mafia. Have you heard of it? No? It is a secret society originating in Sicily that relies on murder and extortion to accomplish its ends. If the Cardinal came here to issue a warning, I suspect it was he who could have used some precautionary advice. But surely he knew the background of Mr Sacco before setting foot in the city. The Pope always knows with whom he is dealing."

As an afterthought, Holmes added: "Upper Swandam Lane after midnight holds plenty of danger on its own without the participation of Mr Sacco."

Holmes sat back down in his armchair, but just before he did he swept his hand across the mantle to grasp the Persian slipper containing his shag tobacco. He filled his black clay pipe and lit the choking mixture, sending acrid clouds of blue smoke hurling toward the ceiling. He then opened one of the windows to let in the refreshing breeze of a fine spring day. "This certainly is more than a one-pipe problem," said he. "Later, we shall call upon the Ambassador and his coachman to see if Lestrade and Company asked them the right questions. Then, a tour of Upper Swandam Lane should be in order."

Before we hailed a cab to take us to Whitehall, where the Ambassador's mansion was nestled among the scattered government buildings, Holmes changed our itinerary and we drove first to Scotland Yard headquarters to see if Lestrade had learned anything beyond what *The Times* had reported.

The inspector came to the lobby to greet us, more warmly than I would have predicted, considering he had guessed the purpose of our calling.

"Well, Mr Holmes, to what do I owe this honour, as if I didn't already know?"

Holmes played along. "Lestrade, I seek your help in the matter of Cardinal Tosca. The Yard is always ready to help the amateur, I have come to realize," said he with exaggerated sarcasm.

"If you tell me where he is hiding, that is all the help I shall need," said Lestrade rather mournfully. "It never ceases to amaze me how many minions can be attracted to the cause of a single big-wig when there is trouble. As it stands, Mr Holmes, we have done all there is to be done and merely are awaiting the next development."

"Have your investigations in Upper Swandam Lane come to anything?" Holmes inquired.

"We have covered the neighbourhood up and down in the daylight and in the dark to find a witness, but it all came to nothing," Lestrade advised. "If anyone saw anything, they're not saying so, which remains a possibility, taking into consideration the low-lifes in that vicinity. None too friendly with the police, and none too eager to cooperate, you know. So, other than to tell you we have come up empty-handed, I have no news."

Our cab rattled through the bustling streets and avenues until it wound its way to Whitehall. For the entire trip, Holmes sat silently, his lips taut and his grey eyes staring blankly at the passing scenery of the dun-coloured buildings. Once, he stirred, and I anticipated that he would make a comment, but he only changed positions and pushed his cloth cap partially over his face. Finally, as we arrived at our destination, he offered a remark—"Most perplexing, Watson"—and stepped down from the cab, sending the driver on his way.

The Ambassador's home abutted the road, a brick and stone edifice with a broad oak door ornamented by shiny hardware. Holmes rapped with the knocker and we waited but a few seconds before an impeccably dressed butler with a long face and grizzled side-whiskers ushered us into a comfortable vestibule with electric lights.

Holmes placed his card on the butler's brass salver and asked if the Ambassador and Monsignor Rossi were at home. With a deep baritone voice, the butler informed him that the Ambassador was occupied in some diplomacy in his study and the Monsignor was expecting him in the library. A footman in a dapper brown tweed suit took us down a long hallway adorned with the portraits of dignitaries, presumably from Italy. We were shown into a large, luxuriously furnished room lined wall to wall with bound volumes. Despite the pleasant temperature outside, there were the embers of a fire in the grate, apparently to discourage dampness in the room, which was encased in stone from the outside. The Monsignor was on a settee awaiting our arrival, and he rose when we entered, closing a Bible as he approached us.

"Welcome. Have you anything to report?" he asked. He was anxious and he nervously fingered the book, demonstrating that he was hoping for good news.

"Only that we have come from Scotland Yard and they are still as baffled as the rest of us," Holmes responded. "Tell me, Monsignor, is it possible that Cardinal Tosca wanted to make himself disappear because of some clandestine aspect to his assignment?"

"Anything is possible, I imagine, but it is highly unlikely," said the Monsignor after a moment of reflection. "This was his first venture into London, so I do not think he was prepared to go off on his own for any length of time."

Then he changed the subject. "I have done as you asked and prepared a history of the Cardinal, dating to the time he was a parish priest," said the Monsignor, walking over to a writing table and withdrawing a sheet of foolscap with script from top to bottom.

"Thank you," said Holmes, taking the biography from the Monsignor and folding it into his notebook after briefly examining the entries. "In the absence of the Ambassador, it would be an efficient use of our time to see the coachman. It is he, so far, who holds the key to our mystery."

Monsignor Rossi led the way to the back of the house. It overlooked a small, neat lawn and immaculate garden, from which a footpath led through laurel bushes to a stable and adjacent paddock. The coachman, wearing his top-hat and waistcoat, was playing cards with the groom and a stable boy at a table just inside the entrance, the doors wide open to take advantage of the glorious weather. The stable was clean and tidy and without an odour, save for the sweet smell of hay. On one wall hung freshly oiled leather—two harnesses, two collars, two bridles and a set of long reins. A pair of bay geldings, fit and well fed, was standing in the stalls watching the card game.

An immigrant, the sour-faced coachman, who was introduced as Pietro Guidotti, spoke broken English, but he seemed to understand the language better when spoken to than when trying to express himself. Monsignor Rossi was forced to act as interpreter for several of Holmes's questions and for many of the answers. Guidotti seemed perturbed for having to handle the same inquiries that the police had posed to him, but there were some questions he had never heard before.

"Did the Cardinal meet anyone when he left the carriage?"

"Yes, a man in working clothes."

"Did the Cardinal speak in English or in Italian to the man?"

"Italiano!" Guidotti proclaimed proudly, gesturing with his fist in the air.

The emotional coachman's barrel chest and bulging, muscled arms were more pronounced now as he stood.

"How did you find Upper Swandam Lane? It is a short, secluded alley, no?"

Guidotti said he knew a woman from that area and had visited her at times.

"Did Cardinal Tosca say why he wanted to go there at such an hour?" Holmes continued.

"He did not say, but it was to minister to the down-trodden, I suppose, since they are awake at night and asleep in the day-time,"

Guidotti answered, seeming to take offense at what appeared to him to be Holmes's implied suggestion that the Cardinal possessed an ulterior motive.

"Did the Cardinal pay you in lira or in pounds?"

"Sir," said Guidotti, "I am a poor boy from Pistoia, but I never would take money from a man of the cloth for doing him a favour. He offered to pay, but when I refused, he thanked me and told me to drive off, so I did."

Holmes concluded the interview by trying to obtain a description of the man in working clothes, but he could get no farther with the coachman. He, therefore, returned to the house to see the Ambassador, who was now free.

Ambassador Arturo Panzini, an aristocrat in manner and in dress, was stoic and helpful. He stroked his straight white hair while he recalled dining with Cardinal Tosca at eight o'clock and entertaining him in the study until about ten, when the Cardinal asked his leave to pray with the servants. The Ambassador said he went to his room and remained there for the night, discovering in the morning that the Cardinal's bed was undisturbed. The Cardinal had mentioned nothing about traveling through the city and had not asked permission to use the brougham.

We were in another cab and well on our way to Baker Street when Holmes said he had decided to forego our trip to Upper Swandam Lane. "I doubt we will have any success where the official police have failed," said he. "It seems more of a job for Shinwell Johnson."

Johnson, who had been Holmes's contact with the underworld after a good-behaviour release from prison, was trusted where the police were regarded with suspicion. He could glean information from the most wretched of characters, his portly and coarse figure a commonplace sight in the worst of places. The inhabitants knew him by the nickname Porky.

Once back in our chambers, Holmes went up to his bedroom and several minutes later emerged into the sitting-room in the garb of a sailor, his pea-jacket opened to expose a turtle-neck jersey. "I'm off, Watson, to locate agent Johnson and give him his assignment. Do remain here in the event Lestrade or the Monsignor attempt to reach me. Respond to them by messenger that I shall return to Baker Street by nine o'clock."

We had not eaten a morsel since breakfast, and so I asked Mrs Hudson to prepare a moderate cold supper, for I was hungry enough that I did not want to wait for something she would have to cook. While she was busy with the supper, I glanced through the *Echo*, which we had picked up from the corner news agent on the way home, to see if there had been any reported new developments in the Cardinal's disappearance. The newspaper was devoid of any mention of the subject. The news was uninteresting: a common burglary, a social event, a government appointment, and many other mundane topics, all reported without a hint of flair or humour. Time dragged until, finally, I heard a key in the latch.

"Shinwell Johnson is on duty," Holmes announced as he came through the door shortly before nine. With a single motion, he seated himself at the table and gathered up some roast beef with two slices of bread that he used to make a sandwich. "I am encouraged, Watson, because Johnson says he knows Upper Swandam Lane like the back of his hand."

When the table was cleared, Holmes stretched out on the sofa with his violin, putting forth dreamy melodies and, alternately, movements or overtures that charged the soul, some of them his own making and others composed by the masters. He kept up the serenade well into the night.

Whether his music-making was therapeutic or an inducement to think about a problem never became clear to me, but it certainly cost me several hours of sleep during the years I shared rooms with Holmes. It was not an unpleasant experience, however, for he had fairly conquered the instrument, and the sounds were cushioned by my bedroom door.

Next morning, I awoke at my usual hour but Holmes already was finishing breakfast. The coffee pot was half empty when I seated myself at the table. "I confess, Watson, that I am confused by the antics of the Cardinal. Unless…" said he, softly, and never completed the sentence. Sherlock Holmes soon curled up in his armchair, smoking a briar root pipe, his knees drawn up to his chin, deep in thought. "A coincidence in this instance is not an occurrence to ignore," said he after a lapse of some five minutes. "In this instance, it is a coincidence on two counts, a coincidence of time and of place. It could mean nothing, or it could mean everything."

The day was another bright and breezy one, which prompted me to suggest a walk through the park. Half way through, Holmes took a route leading to a side street that brought us to the nearest telegraph office, where he sent a wire. "That should shore up one end of this mystery," he declared, and then clapped his bony hands together once.

We had not long to wait for the next development, a more grisly one we had never encountered.

It was about six o'clock when a stout commissionaire delivered a note, obviously scrawled in a hurry. We read it together:

> Mr Holmes:
>   Worst fears materialized. Come to abandoned meat pack-
> er's building in Upper Swandam Lane.
>   Lestrade

In a flash we were in a hansom heading toward the fateful alley. Holmes's whole figure was alert and responsive to every awkward movement of the cab. When we rounded the corner at Regent Street, the sun shone into the passenger compartment and I noted the disappointment in his face.

Soon we were slowing along Fresno Street, where it intersects with Upper Swandam Lane, and then snaking our way along the narrow alley toward the abandoned packing plant. Lestrade, the whites of his beady eyes protruding into the shadow of the building, was pacing out front.

"Some school children playing inside found him, Mr Holmes," Lestrade reported before our feet hit the ground. "It is the Cardinal all right. He's still wearing his cassock and Roman collar, but the rest is almost too gruesome to tell. To think how we've combed this neighborhood backwards and forward, and there he was all along, dead as a doornail."

Holmes glared at the walkway as we approached the interior of the building, making mental notes of the boot impressions on the dusty surface.

"How many men have been in to see the Cardinal? A herd of cattle would not have made a bigger mess!" Holmes bristled, not giving Lestrade an opportunity to respond to an admonishment he had endured before. "Halloa! Halloa! What have we here?" Holmes had noticed two faint parallel lines among the marks of the soles and the heels.

"There are similar ones, Mr Holmes, clearer than these, the farther in you go," said Lestrade. Holmes followed the broken lines to a shocking and horrible scene inside.

The frail body of Cardinal Tosca, his arms drooping and his hands clenched, hung from a meat hook implanted in his back. His swollen tongue parted his lips and extended down toward the pointy chin.

"It is the work of the Black Hand, the Mafia, Mr Holmes, for that's the sign of one who defies the organization—they make him into a side of beef," said Lestrade. "Their message is plain. We'll be fortunate to solve this one, for sure. We know little more now than we did when this was merely a missing person case."

"Don't be so sure, Lestrade," said Holmes matter-of-factly.

"You have a clue, then?" Lestrade begged.

"I have a line of inquiry, an indication, and it is far too premature for me to discuss here," Holmes responded. He whipped a convex lens along with a tape measure out of his jacket pocket to begin a meticulous examination of the area and the corpse.

The light had gone out of the room and Holmes called for dark-lanterns from the policemen milling about outside. He began his examination on his knees, mumbling to himself. He was down on the ground for ten minutes at least, making notes and moving about the area in such a way that he was careful not to disturb any evidence. Once he shouted "Voila!" and said nothing more that our ears could discern, save for the mumbling.

Next, he called again for the constables, this time to remove the body from the hook and lay it on the stone floor. They did so gently, with reverence. Holmes pried open one of the fists and with great pains he scrutinized the nails with his lens. Finally, he withdrew his penknife, took a small envelope from his inside breast pocket, scraped underneath the nails of the middle finger and the ring finger, and deposited some minute debris into the container, which he returned to his breast pocket. Then he repeated the process with the other fist.

Afterward, he took several minutes examining the throat, once taking his index finger and rubbing it along the blue line that a garrote had caused, for the victim had been strangled. He took his index finger and held it under his nose to smell it, as if some substance had adhered. "Remarkable," said he, but nothing more.

Lestrade and I watched from the background while the artist constructed his masterpiece, ignoring his surroundings, isolated from the rest of the world. In the end, he got back up on his feet and addressed Lestrade:

"This dreadful crime was committed by one man only, not a gang of men, a very strong man over six feet in height and wearing a size twelve boot with a square toe. I have calculated his height by measuring the length of his stride and the distance from the ground to the hook. The murder took place somewhere other than this meat packer's shop. The body was dragged here after the Cardinal was dead, for there's no mark of his own boot anywhere on the ground, only the backs of his heels. Robbery is a possible motive, for his purse is empty, unless that's a blind to throw you off the scent. I suspect a blind because only a venomous bandit would go to such a length as to hang his victim by a meat hook."

"Well, Mr Holmes, that gives us a start, but it doesn't rule out the killer being hired by the Mafia. This fellow Sacco could have ordered the execution after the Cardinal paid him a visit," Lestrade asserted confidently.

"Do pursue that line of inquiry, Lestrade, and I shall pursue mine, until one of us shows the other how it was done and by whom," said Holmes.

With that we departed, my sympathies flowing to the devoted Monsignor Rossi, while I wondered aloud to Holmes how the priest would accept the news of the Cardinal's tragic end.

All night, Holmes, clad in his mouse-coloured dressing gown, paced the floor, his chin on his chest, his brows furrowed, and his hands clasped behind his back. He was in that condition when I went to bed and in the same condition when I awakened the next morning, but more agitated. He criticized the results of my shaving and my choice of a necktie. "Please pardon my temperament, Watson. My irritability will soon end, however," said he. "By today we should know something positive." I poured a cup of coffee and settled in at the table with the newspaper to see what version of events it contained. There were details of the murder missing from the account, but the writer was nonetheless ready to attribute the killing to a robber. I read the article aloud to Holmes.

"The newsies have jumped to an erroneous conclusion, as usual," he observed, amused by the situation.

A little later there was a ring at the bell, followed by a patter of light footsteps on the stairs, and then a light knock at the door. "It is undoubtedly one of the Baker Street Irregulars," Holmes guessed, and sure enough an overwrought street Arab who was one of Holmes's spies appeared on the threshold when he opened the door. "Come in, Andrew, and tell us what all the excitement is about."

"I have come with word from Mr Shinwell Johnson," said the lad. "He wants to see you as soon as possible at the Rialto Café on Leadenhall Street near the post office." Holmes tossed the boy a shilling from the mantel and went to his room to change into the sailor clothes. "I shall return when I return, Watson, for there is no telling what Porky Johnson has unearthed," said Holmes when he came down from the bedroom. "I would invite you to join me but it would arouse suspicions if two were seen discussing business with him," he explained on his way out the door. "I knew today would bring us a fresh avenue," I heard him say as I closed the door and his feet were on the stairs.

It was an opportune time for me to catch up on my medical journals. There was an article about the treatment of brain fever that I was particularly interested in reading. Nevertheless, time passed slowly.

About three o'clock, a messenger delivered a note.

> Watson (it read):
> Join me for a glass of claret at Simpson's.
> S H

I put on my waterproof, for it had begun to rain hard shortly after Holmes's departure, and I took a cab to our favourite restaurant in the Strand. Holmes had a table by the window and was smoking a cigarette, a wine bottle and two glasses in front of him. "I have already christened the bottle, with your indulgence, my friend," said he. I poured myself a glass and could not resist asking how the case was progressing, seeing a brightness in Holmes's expression.

"It is solved," said he, "except for a few loose ends—one that will require my making a trip to the Continent."

I knew better than to ask the solution before Holmes was ready to divulge the information. "Shinwell Johnson has provided the key evidence, then?" I asked instead.

"Hardly so, Watson. I had deduced the outcome when I examined the body of the Cardinal. Johnson, simply put, has confirmed it."

Holmes was gone almost three days, and when he came back the expression on his gaunt face had changed to a sternness that foretold a grim ending. I met him at Waterloo Station the afternoon of the third day and we hurried to the office of a messenger service before it closed. He sent word to Ambassador Panzini and Lestrade, instructing them to meet him at ten o'clock in the morning at Baker Street. Monsignor Rossi already had left London, accompanying the remains of Cardinal Tosca back to Rome for burial.

"Our client at the Vatican is not going to appreciate the resolution of this matter," said Holmes as we awaited the arrival of the Ambassador's brougham. Lestrade, who came about a half hour early, chided Holmes for his penchant toward the dramatic. "Why don't you just tell us what you know and be done with it?" he complained.

"Did you bring the three strong constables as I instructed?" asked Holmes.

"Yes, they are standing down at the corner, as you can see from your window," Lestrade replied.

Holmes pulled back the curtain and double-checked, nodding his approval.

"Here is the Ambassador now," said he. "I dare say Mrs Hudson was expecting him—she has the door opened before he is even out of the carriage," Holmes remarked wryly.

In a minute, the elegantly dressed diplomat stood in the doorway, fixing his cuffs and straightening his collar. He was all formality as he introduced his assistant, Angelo Saccani.

"I presume you have fresh word of the Cardinal's murder," the Ambassador intoned.

"I see you have brought along the murderer," said Holmes with coolness.

"What? What is the meaning of this?" the Ambassador demanded, glancing at his aide.

"No, no, not him!" Holmes answered, smiling. "It is he, Pietro Guidotti, who killed Cardinal Tosca," cried Holmes as he went to the window and pointed at the huge coachman.

"Perhaps you should explain this theory of yours, Mr Holmes, before we get too excited," said an unconvinced Lestrade.

"I shall, in due course, Inspector," said Holmes, "but do you not think the constables should take him into custody first?"

"I'll send them onto him after I blow this whistle," Lestrade replied.

"Very well," said Holmes. "Let me enumerate the facts that will persuade a jury to render a verdict of guilty.

"First of all, Guidotti and the Cardinal go back a long way together. Guidotti was born and raised in Pistoia, a village north of Florence near the Swiss border. It so happens that Pistoia is the place Cardinal Tosca was assigned as a parish priest after his ordination, according to a biography furnished by Monsignor Rossi. Such a coincidence was too suspicious to ignore, and it led to the discovery of a sinister relationship when I traveled to the Continent.

"Something terrible occurred in Pistoia when Guidotti was nine years old and serving as an acolyte at Mother of Sorrows Church for young Father Tosca.

"Knowing there was this connection between the two, I sent a wire to the pastor there now, asking what might cause Guidotti to harbour ill will toward the Cardinal. I received an intriguing reply, saying only that the coachman's parents might shed some light on the topic. I took the pastor at his word and journeyed to Pistoia, learning from the Guidottis that their son, when he was nine, made an accusation that the young Father Tosca molested him. They recalled how the boy sobbed bitterly when he told the story, but they do not believe it to this day. They attribute the story to an over-active imagination and a need for attention.

"Revenge is the motive here, revenge for an abuse that Guidotti has endured alone since childhood, unable to share its abominable consequences even with his skeptical mother and father.

"During my investigation of the body of Cardinal Tosca, I noticed two peculiarities. The first was that he had shards of hay under his nails on both hands, indicating that in his agony he grasped at whatever was in front of him. Secondly, there was a deposit of oil on his neck, which likely came from a set of leather reins in the Ambassador's stable. It was there, I concluded, that the murder was done and that the whole idea of the Cardinal asking for a ride to Upper Swandam Lane was fabricated by the coachman. The Cardinal had never been to London, so how could he have known the streets so intimately? None of the coachman's statements had the ring of truth, which is the reason I asked certain questions of Guidotti that gave him the chance to make up more preposterous lies than he told to the police.

"After he killed the Cardinal, Guidotti deposited the body onto the floor of the brougham, which he drove to the familiar alley near London Bridge. Still in a fit of rage, he used his great strength and height to hang the Cardinal on a meat hook to avenge the molestation and the years of bearing the burden alone. He next took the Cardinal's money and calmly walked out of the building.

"One of my agents has located a prostitute who remembers seeing the coachman, an occasional customer at her brothel, going from the building to the brougham about midnight on Tuesday last. She had just come out of the house to have a cigarette on the back stoop because the madam forbids smoking inside. She recognized the coachman when he went into the light of a lantern on the side of the carriage. She also recognized the horses.

"It is conjecture on my part, but it can be verified—if Guidotti talks—that when the Cardinal went to the stable that night to say prayers he didn't recognize Guidotti, who is now a middle-aged man. But Guidotti obviously knew the Cardinal and probably heard his name mentioned as a guest by the servants. It is more than likely that Guidotti revealed his identity to the Cardinal, probably in the last remaining moment of his life.

"Have I failed to make any of the events clear?"

"Only on one point am I confused," said Lestrade. "How came the Cardinal and Guidotti to be in the stable so late at night?"

Holmes provided this explanation:

"About ten-thirty is the hour when Guidotti prepares to retire, and he goes to the stable to replenish the water buckets and fill the hay racks for the last time. That is his habit, according to my agent, who conducted a surveillance of the coachman from the laurel bushes. It was about ten-thirty when the Cardinal would have finished praying with the servants in the house. He made the stable his next stop. If the coachman had not been there, chances were that a light still would be burning in the apartment."

Without a word, Lestrade went to the window. He lifted the latch and opened it.

Then he blew three times on his whistle.

LAST MAN STANDING

by Dianne Ell

Anticipating a great weekend in the Hamptons and the rolling greens of the Atlantic Golf Course, Howard Frazier had risen earlier than usual. Buoyed by the blue skies visible through the early morning mist rising above the Hudson River, he finished his last minute packing. At six forty-five on that first Friday in May, he left his West End Avenue apartment for the garage and by a little after seven was in his office on the fortieth floor of the United Broadcasting Systems building overlooking Rockefeller Center.

As Executive Vice President of News and Sports for the media giant UBS, as it was known, Frazier's day began without variation whether he was in the office or on the road. The routine gave order to his day and an advantage over the competition. Having been in the business a long time, he had fingers into all the nooks and crannies where news could originate, whether it was in Miami, Malaysia, or Moscow, and having sophisticated electronic roadways that connected field reporters to New York, made him, and UBS, number one.

He got his cup of coffee, sat in his usual comfortable chair and turned on the six television monitors that spanned the side wall. First he reviewed the loglines and clips for each of the shows where news would be running: the morning show, post morning show, local, national, and international news programs. Then he read through the stories that were under development. He saw nothing that would give him anxious moments over the weekend, or worse, cause him to cancel his plans altogether.

When he finished, he stood, stretched, then walked back to the coffee pot to refill his cup halfway. He had one last news update system to go through. The one that logged in the phone calls and emails that came in from ordinary folks during what the news department called the 'zombie hours'—eleven p.m. to six a.m. If anything of interest was in the log, the reporter who picked up the story would leave one. There were no messages which made it tempting to skip the last step. But as he watched the rays of the early morning sun slide across the floor and up the side of his desk, an instinct born of years in the business told him not to.

Taking his coffee, he settled at his desk and opened the program to review the night's calls. Later, when he looked back on that moment, it was the trivial things he would remember…what he was planning, the day's temperature, the sky's color, what he was wearing. Even as he began to read, he had no idea how quickly his day would disintegrate. Pandora's Box was child's play.

The calls that came in between the hours of eleven-thirty to two-thirty a.m. were the kind they usually received at that time of night: bar brawls, prostitutes on Eighth Avenue, neighbor dogs barking, theft at an all-night drug store and so on. Every call received a followup. It was amazing what people thought was newsworthy. They needed to do a program on that. It was when he reached the call that came in at 3:22, that his heart nearly stopped.

The caller was Frank Holzer. A name he hoped never to see again in this lifetime. The 'reason for calling' was not mentioned, but he left his location as the Catskills. Same person who caused him nightmares back at the Winter Games in Innsbruck had returned.

He tried not to panic. It was not in his nature. He was too old a newsman to be rattled. And while he didn't know the nature of the call, he could make a guess. He hoped he was wrong.

To compound the problem, the call was picked up by Meg Worth. Her handling of it would be worse than an A-bomb being detonated. As a former secret service agent she saw herself as a network news personality and used connections to get a coveted spot as a junior reporter for domestic news—over his objections. She didn't understand the protocol that went into developing and handling news stories and was too busy scrambling to get to the top to learn. If she picked up the call on Holzer at five thirty, where was it? He reviewed stories under development and it wasn't listed for local or national news. What was she doing with it?

He rubbed the bottom of his chin as he thought. Nothing he could imagine made any sense. As much as he hated to, he picked up the phone and dialed her number. No answer. Maybe there was nothing. He was letting the memories of Innsbruck get the better of him. Then again, Holzer wouldn't be calling the network in the middle of the night because he had nothing better to do.

Frazier stood, then paced the room. Where else would she go with it? As he stared at the trophies and awards for news excellence lining the shelves on the opposite wall, he had the answer. Weekend News…Jim Regan's department.

He looked at the time. A half-hour from now, Regan's *Weekend Edition* team would meet and spend the morning deciding what stories would fill the Saturday and Sunday broadcasting hours. The program handled late breaking news, but as research discovered, the audience turned in for the amusing, lighthearted, and mostly off-beat news stories that the team spent the week gathering. Since *Weekend Edition* didn't air until Saturday at noon, Regan didn't post the loglines in advance. This was the only place left for Meg and Frank Holzer.

At eight forty-five, Frazier put aside the work he was doing, slipped into his suit jacket which hid the circle of flesh that was causing his belt to expand, loosened his tie, checked his dark hair that seemed to be threaded with more and more gray, and headed for the conference room. He entered from the rear and took a seat at the table next to Regan.

A few weeks had passed since the last time he sat in on one of Regan's meetings. It was good to see that UBS's renovation team finally made their way to this spot after five years of requests. Gone were the depressing beige walls, the moldy-looking green carpet and beige colored chairs. Now the walls were a tranquil blue and the chairs had a striped pattern that sort of matched the walls and new carpet. It was good for him. He hoped it was for everyone else.

"What brings you here?" Regan asked, looking at his boss. Regan was about six foot, gray hair, and a build that suggested his down time was spent in the gym.

"Searching for the cave of the Minotaur." Frazier looked around the room. One of the smaller conference rooms, the table sat twenty people and it seemed as though all seats would be taken. He noticed that a few of the men who had been slouching, sat up straight as they saw him.

"Minotaur?" Regan opened his laptop and turned it on. "What are you following to get there?"

"A phone call that appeared on last night's call-in report. It went to Meg Worth." At the mention of her name, Frazier could see Regan's features tighten. "It wasn't on the logs for any of the morning news programs and it didn't appear in the stories under development, so you were my last hope."

"Why are you tracking it?" Regan looked at him.

"The call was from Frank Holzer."

At the sound of the name, a strange puzzled look came over Regan's face. "Holzer?" Regan began to pass around the typed sheets with the list of the stories to be discussed. He nodded his head. "Refresh my memory."

Frazier moved closer to Regan and lowered his voice. "Saturday night in Innsbruck before the games opened, a guy by the name of Harmon Thatcher tried to steal one of our experimental cameras. Multi-million dollar theft. He was a member of the U.S. Bobsled Team. Needed money. Anyway, remember, we caught him with the camera and brought him back to the control center. He claimed someone paid him fifty thousand to steal it. We thought he might have been lying, but he showed us a hand-drawn map and the key to the cabinet where the camera was kept."

"What happened to him?"

"Weren't you around the control room that night?" It was Frazier's turn to look puzzled.

"I was in town. We had just finished wrapping a story on how Innsbruck handles the Olympics. Only heard the Thatcher story in bits and piece. So, what happened to him?"

"We had the camera, and the first of the bobsled events was on the Sunday schedule. Some folks wanted to let Thatcher go. But our new commander-in-chief, the guy who sits in the corner office down the hall from me, chatted with both the local police and the embassy who set up a small office in Innsbruck for the Olympics. The local police saw it as our problem. The embassy wasn't sure. So everyone decided that since it was late, after midnight, we'd deal with it in the morning. We gave Thatcher a room at the main hotel and had security watch over him."

"That's right. Thatcher disappeared, didn't he?"

"Yeah. He picked the lock on the hotel room door. Can you beat that? He walked away around noon on that Sunday and disappeared. Been three months and he still hasn't shown. We know

Thatcher didn't leave the country under his name so where is he? Still hiding out, or dead? We needed him to tell us who hired him. Had to be a UBS employee. Possibly a contractor, but I don't think so."

"Where does Holzer fit in?"

"He and Thatcher were roommates," Frazier replied. "We think he was meeting Holzer outside the hotel that Sunday afternoon. If so, he would have known what happened. We hoped he'd come forth with the truth. Save his friend. Save the team. That kind of thing. Except it didn't happen. After three months, he must have had some kind of epiphany to call us in the middle of the night."

"And Meg Worth picked up the story? You think she's going to show up here. Last minute."

"There she is." Frazier looked at the entrance.

They watched as the tall, good-looking blonde dressed in a red and navy suit spoke to the man who assembled the stories for this morning.

"Hard to believe she was Secret Service. Can you imagine her with a gun?" Regan shook his head. "She doesn't seem all that together."

"Let's see how good she is at hitting the target with Holzer."

The man who was assembling the stories kept shaking his head as Meg spoke. Finally he pointed across the room. She followed his finger and her expression froze.

"Gotcha," Frazier said to Regan. "Let's find out what she's up to. Why don't you start the meeting?"

Regan stood and got everyone's attention. He quickly went over the rules for story submission then said, "Rather than go through today's list in alphabetical order, I'm going to call the stories at random."

He chose two from the middle of the list and one from the end, then turned his attention to Meg Worth. "You're not on the schedule, which you know is against the rules. But since Frazier is here I'll make an exception What do you have?"

"I'd like to run with a story about Frank Holzer," Meg said.

Regan looked through the computer at past titles. "We ran something on Holzer at the time of the Olympics. There wasn't anything else press-worthy about him. What's different about your story?"

"I spoke to Frank Holzer an hour ago. His teammate disappeared at the beginning of the Olympics. The story got hushed up. Holzer says he's now ready to talk about it."

Regan glanced at Frazier. "Why don't you take this? Better you tangle with her than me."

Frazier nodded. "I was there," he said to her, leaning forward. "Holzer had his chance. At the time he had nothing to say. Not to me, not to Thad Bannen who runs UBS, not to the Innsbruck police, and not to the American Embassy. So what does he have now that he didn't have then?"

She cleared her throat. "He has photos. Holzer was parked across the street from the hotel. While he was waiting for Thatcher to come out, he took pics of the area. As he was snapping away, he caught not only Thatcher coming down the steps but the people who met him."

Frazier coughed and grabbed at the glass of water in front of him. "What happened after that? He never got in the car with Holzer, otherwise he wouldn't be missing."

"Something's wrong here," Regan said leaning over. "She's not reading the situation. Are you sure she was secret service?"

Frazier sighed deeply. "I'll take this one." He stood. "We're going to let Jim get on with his meeting," he said, addressing Meg. "We'll go to the conference room next door and continue this discussion."

Meg stood her ground. "Am I getting on the air with this or not?"

Regan spoke up. "You don't have a story yet. Until you do, we'll put it in the 'under development' category."

Angrily, Meg picked up her papers and walked toward Frazier with a venomous look.

He headed out the door and led the way to a room across the hall. Once inside, he closed the door and leaned against the conference room table, doing the best he could to keep his temper under control.

"Who knows Holzer contacted us? I mean besides everyone who was in that room, the camera team you've undoubtedly lined up, and all the folks in between you've mentioned this to."

Meg looked uncomfortable. "Maybe a dozen."

"Why didn't you come to me with this story?" Frazier asked. "That's the procedure."

"You would have assigned it to someone else. I'm ready to handle this," she argued.

Frazier looked thoughtfully at her. The hell she was. "What else did Holzer say?"

She hesitated. "He followed the car that Thatcher got into."

That, he hadn't expected. "And…"

"He saw Thatcher murdered."

"Murdered?" Frazier blinked hard. "He saw it. He can identify who did it?"

"He said he can identify one of the men and the car."

"What were you planning to do with this information?" Frazier kept the tenor of his voice on an even keel. "And what did you plan to do with Holzer? Didn't it occur to you that if he has photos of the killer he's putting his life in danger by coming forward? Why didn't you head up to his place this morning to see what he had?"

"I wanted to make certain I had a time slot to air his story."

No sense of anything. All she was interested in was being an on-air personality. The story before the man's life. "And let's say you get it. Then what?"

"He said to come Sunday. He owns an auto repair shop and Friday and Saturday are busy days. On Sunday, I want to take a crew to the Catskills where he lives and go 'live' from there."

Frazier was so angry he could have put his fist through the conference room table. He shook his head at the stupidity of the reasoning. She didn't get it. She never would.

"Get the story. Bring it back here. Then we'll decide how it airs. And make it tomorrow early. I don't care what Holzer wants. He came to us. He plays by our rules." Frazier walked out of the room, calling over his shoulder. "And only one cameraman. You interview. He films. More than that comes out of your salary."

He returned to his office. The encounter left him with a surreal feeling. The half-dozen people who had been involved with that Sunday at the Olympics fiasco had probably forgotten about it except for himself and the guy in the corner office Thad Bannen. He could tell him now. He could tell him later. Later was better.

Staring out the window, he thought about what came next. He could see his long anticipated weekend plans going south. Since he didn't trust Meg to do the right thing, he needed to get there first and find out exactly what Holzer knew. And he needed to take his own advice and keep his trip secret. A search of Olympic files told him that Holzer lived in Big Indian. And a look at the New York State map gave him directions. It was now about eleven. He could be in Big Indian by mid afternoon.

Even though it was May, it was still early spring in the mountains. The apple orchards, hardwood trees, and open fields, rubbed bare by the raw winter winds were just beginning to sprout their spring finery. As the two-lane highway rose over the increasingly higher elevations of the Catskills, the fields gave way to thick evergreen forests and rock-faced mountain peaks. In serpentine fashion, the road continued its ascent as it ran alongside the Esopus River, past the ski centers, then finally west into Big Indian.

It was nearly three-thirty by the time Howard Frazier reached the town. He stopped at the gas station Holzer owned. He filled his tank, then before going inside glanced momentarily at his reflection in the glass portion of the door. A change of clothes and a stop in the prop department provided him with a baseball cap, sunglasses, and a mustache. Just enough of a disguise in case someone had a need to remember. Before paying, he took off his driving gloves, laid them on the counter, then removed his wallet from his pants pocket. As he paid the man behind the counter, he said, "I see the name Holzer. Any relation to the man who competed in the Olympics?"

"The same," the gray-haired man said with a broad smile.

"I stay at the Beacon Lodge every year about this time to do some fishing and just generally get away from it," Frazier remarked of the lodge a few miles to the west, well-known as a mecca for sportsmen. "I've stopped in here before for gas. Never noticed the sign."

"Many people around here didn't know Frank competed. Shows you what a little publicity will do." Being careful, Frazier pocketed the change, then put the gloves back on.

Before he left, Frazier learned a lot about Frank's routine, where he lived, and a little about Meg's interview, which wasn't the secret he hoped it to be.

By the time he turned into the road leading to Holzer's home, the sun was on the afternoon slide, leaving the heavily treed area in muted sunlight. At the end of the graveled area, he found the house. It was a type of split-level made of wood overlooking the lake. A balcony wrapped around the back of the house and opened onto a deck built atop the three-car garage. The door to the garage was closed. He climbed the stairs to the first floor and rang the bell.

When a minute passed and no one answered, he rang the bell again. The air was so still he could hear fish jump in the lake. Where was Holzer? He fumed as he waited. He peered in the windows. He could see a living room and beyond it, a kitchen. He followed the balcony around until he reached the deck above the garage. From here, he could see the lake through the leafy branches of the trees. It was very quiet. Opening onto this side of the deck was a sliding glass door. He tested it and to his surprise it slid back. He called to Holzer.

Getting no reply, he stepped inside and found himself in a large kitchen with a built-in dining area. Clean. No pots, pans, or dishes showing. He called again then walked in the direction of the living room where country music was playing. The room had two walls which were paneled, and two were painted a deep green. In the middle of the far wall was a large fireplace with smoldering embers.

"Frank," Frazier called out once more. As he looked around the room, he noticed a glass partially filled with amber liquid sitting on top of the end table. He went over and smelled it. Whiskey. The ice cubes had melted but the glass was still cool. Wherever Holzer went, he intended to come back soon.

Frazier returned to the deck. Once outside in the chilly late afternoon air, he walked to the edge of the deck and carefully surveyed the property. As he stood at the railing, he looked out over the leaf covered ground then his gaze followed the shoreline of the lake. About seventy-five yards away was a building. Probably a boathouse.

Curious, Frazier retraced his steps around the balcony and started down the stairs when it occurred to him to check the garage to see if any vehicles were missing. The man at the gas station indicated that Holzer was home, but maybe he had to duck out for a few minutes. He went down the stairs where he found a Ram

1500, a Jeep Cherokee, and a Harley. Wherever Holzer had gone, he wasn't driving.

As he made his way to the outside, the breeze kicked up and the chill of night began to set in. He was beginning to get a very bad feeling. Something unexpected interrupted Holzer's afternoon. He got his gun and flashlight out of the car then headed for the boathouse. Rather than take the gravel path to the lake then follow the shoreline where he'd be out in the open, he decided to take a few minutes longer and cut through the trees and the underbrush. This way, if he had asked too many questions in the gas station and Holzer was alerted to his coming, he wouldn't see his approach.

When Frazier reached the boathouse, the sun was making one last magnanimous gesture. Rays of golden light burst forth through the clouds and floated momentarily on the placid water. Then it was gone and all that was left was orange and purple residue.

There were three doors into the boathouse—two large doors by which the boat left and returned, and the usual one for pedestrian traffic. It was that door which was slightly ajar. Suddenly, the hairs stood up on his arms. Frazier removed his gloves and took out his gun. He leaned against the door and listened. He heard nothing. Not even a breeze crackling the dry wood. Years of instinct suddenly gathered forces, but he had no inkling as to what was wrong. Was Holzer inside waiting for him, gun ready?

He called out. The only sound was the rushing of the wind through the pines. He pushed the door open, then crouched against it as he looked inside. The boat loomed in the foreground, a dark silhouette against a black background. As he quickly surveyed the room, in the fading light he thought he saw something on the wooden floor near the boat. He lowered himself to the floor and crawled inside. The door closed silently behind him, leaving the barest sliver of light to cut the darkness. Frazier remained motionless. The only sound was the water slapping against the floor's opening.

Finally, convinced he was alone, he turned on the flashlight. Almost directly ahead of him was a dark-haired man laying face down, one leg on the wooden plank, one leg hanging over the edge, his head barely elevated above the darkened water of the boat ramp. He crawled closer and saw that blood had coagulated from the bullet wound in the back of his head. Frazier reached over and touched his wrist. The skin and hand were still flexible, so Holzer hadn't been dead very long. Judging by the drink that was left on the end table and the glowing embers, he was willing to bet perhaps less than a half hour. Just before he arrived. He glanced at his watch. It was nearly six.

Frazier started to stand when he felt the presence of someone behind him. Suddenly, it all became very clear. How could he have been so dumb? He knew someone didn't want Holzer telling what he knew and had been waiting for the right time to get him. If only he had been quicker. Better. He criticized himself for not anticipating this, for losing the edge that made the difference between life and death. The only question that lingered now was would he be able to get off at least one shot? Or would he die as lamely as Holzer?

Survival techniques long out of use quickly passed through his brain. He pulled into play what he remembered. Without turning around, he listened and looked directly ahead toward Holzer's body. From the way the remaining light fell into the boathouse, he knew that the person behind him was a little to the left against the opened door. He had only another couple of seconds of life left while the intruder waited for him to react. *Make a guess*, he thought. *And it better be a good one*. Without warning, he shifted his weight to the right, spun around and fired as he dropped to the floor.

The intruder's bullet missed him. He didn't know if his found its mark but the door clanged shut and for what seemed like an eternity Frazier remained next to the inert body of Frank Holzer. Then he got up and moved cautiously across the floor. He leaned against the door jamb and listened. There were no sounds. Was his assailant still out there? He turned on his flashlight and found a large stone on the floor. He threw it out the partially-opened doorway and as it hit the ground, he heard the soft pop of a silencer. He had his answer.

Seeing no choice, Frazier settled on the floor to wait. He thought back to this morning and his weekend plans. This was not what he had in mind.

About ten minutes later, he heard the nearby sound of a car engine. Taking a chance, he opened the door and slipped outside. The soft purple of evening dusted everything. There was just enough light left for Frazier to find his way through the woods to the dirt road.

He reached it just as the dark profile of the car pulled out from behind a group of trees, heading away from him toward the highway. Even in the fading light he recognized the car. He hated knowing his instincts were right. Being alone here wasn't safe. The driver could return. The breeze whispered, telling him to go.

For a fleeting moment he thought of reporting Holzer's death, then decided nothing could be gained from it. It would open a can of worms of gargantuan proportions. Besides, there was nothing he could do for him, anyway. The time for that was yesterday or the day before. Or never.

Unless someone had taken down his license plate number when he stopped at the gas station, which he doubted, no one except Holzer's killer knew he had made the journey to Big Indian. He walked to where he had parked his car and began the long drive back to New York.

If there was any consolation in what happened, it was that Meg Worth would not get her story. And that no doubt she needed to take at least partial responsibility for Holzer's death. It reminded him of Benjamin Franklin's saying: 'three can keep a secret if two are dead'. Thatcher and Holzer were. Only the third man was left and Frazier intended to go after him. How could he not have seen it. Army buddies. Years of working together. Why? He only wished it hadn't been Jim Regan.

✗

COLONEL WARBURTON'S MADNESS

by Sasscer Hill

In the summer of 1890, not long after my marriage, I had returned to private practice, leaving Sherlock Holmes alone in our old Baker Street rooms. I had been exceptionally busy that summer and consequently felt rather nervy and rundown. So much so that Mary, my wife, persuaded me to take a fortnight's holiday in the charming little village of Taplow on the lower reaches of the Thames.

I had left Holmes in a bad state in London. With no puzzle or case to occupy his mind, he had once again turned to artificial stimulants, which inevitably brought on a black moodiness. Had I not been concerned for my own health and my wife's happiness, I would have been reluctant to leave him.

However, a most peculiar event occurred that allowed me to write to Holmes asking for his advice after we had been in Taplow only a few days.

Mary and I had been enjoying a walk as the day was particularly balmy. Birds were singing, and the sun shone on the park by the river where we strolled. We had just skirted a flock of geese when Mary noticed a figure heading in our direction.

"Oh, John, look," she said. "Do you see that woman walking across the fields toward us?"

"What is it, dear? Do you know her?"

"I'm not certain, but I think it is Ellen Warburton. I believe she does live somewhere near here."

"And who is Ellen Warburton?" I asked.

"An old friend of mine. She is frightfully clever and advanced, and believes in women's suffrage and all sorts of progressive things."

"Most interesting," I said.

As Mary's friend drew closer, I made out the features and figure of a woman about thirty, with light chestnut hair, unremarkable eyes, and a rather small mouth.

"It is Ellen," Mary said eagerly. Waving, she stepped forward. "Ellen!"

Miss Warburton reached us, and after making introductions, she and Mary chatted amiably, catching up on events since they had last met. A brief study of Miss Warburton's face led me to believe some worry or fear plagued her. But these thoughts were interrupted by Mary.

With a glow I can only describe as pride, she said, "Imagine, I am Mary Watson now."

"I heard you'd married." Miss Warburton said, her eyes lingering on me a moment. "And you are a medical detective or something, Doctor Watson?"

Mary giggled. "Not quite, Ellen."

I said, "I hold a degree of Doctor of Medicine from the University of London, madam."

Mary's fingers brushed my forearm a moment. "But John has helped the great Sherlock Holmes on many of his cases."

"Ah, that's how I have heard of you, then. But you are back in private practice now?"

"Yes," I replied. "The work keeps me busy, and I don't see so much of Holmes these days."

Miss Warburton nodded. "Do you mind if I walk with you a little way?"

"Of course not, Ellen, come along." Mary linked her arm through Miss Warburton's.

"Do you live near here, Miss Warburton?" I asked.

"Yes, about four miles away, at Chevy Grange." Miss Warburton's gaze moved beyond us, to the river.

An excursion steamboat worked its way up the Thames. A number of people on the vessel's deck sat or stood beneath an awning. The breeze carried the faint sound of their laughter.

"I keep house for my uncle," Miss Warburton said.

"The uncle who went to Africa?" Mary asked.

"Yes, Colonel Warburton. He's recently returned to England, and I have moved to Chevy Grange." Miss Warburton's voice faltered. "I don't want to burden you…"

"What's the matter?" Mary stopped abruptly.

"My uncle…" She paused, then seemed to gather herself. "He is going mad before my eyes, and I can do nothing to help him."

Miss Warburton's voice carried a desperate note. "That's why I asked if I might walk with you."

"Surely you exaggerate? *Mad?*" Mary's kind eyes filled with compassion.

"What are the symptoms, Miss Warburton?" I asked, trying to keep my own doubt from my voice.

"Doctor, I am not an hysterical girl. In fact, I regard myself as something of a scientist. Uncle encouraged me to study under Professor Thompson at University College, Bristol. Among other things, I studied physics. I tell you my uncle is going insane."

Miss Warburton had worked herself into quite a state. "Why don't we sit for a moment?" I gestured at a painted bench deep in the shade of a tall oak. "I should like to hear more about his condition, Miss Warburton."

After we were seated, Miss Warburton turned to me. "Most of the time he is perfectly normal, but when these attacks are upon him, he falls into frightful rages and says the strangest things. He has even complained of some shrill, painful sound that he says comes out of nowhere. I cannot hear it, nor can anyone else." Miss Warburton clasped her hands together, and her face tightened in distress.

"Curious," I murmured.

"Uncle gets into the most dreadful state. I wonder, would you have a look at him for me, Doctor Watson?"

"Well, I don't know…"

"Of course, John will do everything he can." Mary delivered a meaningful look in my direction.

"Oh, thank you so much." Miss Warburton pressed her slender hands together.

"I'm sure Uncle would be happy to have company for dinner. Perhaps you both would call on us this evening?"

And so, we found ourselves approaching Chevy Grange at seven that evening. I must confess, I was not entirely pleased with the idea, nor with the appearance of Colonel Warburton's home.

Though the house stood on a pleasant enough rise, the sun had dropped low on the horizon behind it. Tall crooked chimneys and a towering slate roof cast long grey shadows into which we walked. Ancient stone blocks appeared dark and damp, and the windows were oddly narrow. Glancing around the grounds, I found the woodlands grew too close for my liking.

"Gloomy looking place, isn't it?" I said to Mary.

"It is a bit foreboding." She looked about uneasily as we climbed cold stone steps to the solid entry door.

I raised the brass knocker and let it fall several times. A hollow sound echoed from within. Then a peculiar, repetitive singing or wailing reached us from beyond a small stand of trees to our right.

"What is that?" Mary asked.

"Sounds like drums, and someone singing a weird chant. Seems to be coming from the building over there, probably the carriage house."

"Yes," agreed Mary. "I see the stable beyond it. But who would be beating drums?"

Through the trees, a faint light flickered from a window in the carriage house.

"Doesn't seem quite appropriate, does it?" Mary said. "Especially in the heart of Buckinghamshire. Should you knock again, John?"

"Perhaps they did not hear us," I said, rapping with more energy.

The sudden sound of bolts sliding back startled me. The door swung open to reveal a short manservant with stumpy legs, a long, pointed nose, and grey hair in need of a barber's attention.

"Who is it?" his voice rasped. "Ow, guests, is it?"

"I am Dr John H Watson, and this is my wife."

"Ah…you are expected, sir."

Though the man bobbed his head, I found his attitude somehow insulting.

He continued, "The Colonel is in the library. This way, if you please."

As we followed the manservant down a dark stone hall, I said, "Just now, as we were waiting outside the front door, we heard a strange chant. It sounded as if someone was beating drums."

"Oh, that would be Miss Nada, sir." He seemed disinclined to elaborate as he led us through the hall.

He showed us into the library, and Colonel Warburton rose from his chair to greet us. He looked well enough, and I would have known him for a military man without his title. His ramrod posture and air of confidence were unmistakable evidence of a career in service.

I glanced around. African spears, leopard skins, and other trophies lined the wall behind him. Bookcases filled with leather-bound volumes filled two walls, and oil paintings flanking a large fireplace made up the last.

"May I offer you a sherry, Mrs Watson?" he asked.

Mary readily accepted, and as I agreed to a whisky, I noticed a small table with a brandy decanter and a half-filled glass placed next to the Colonel's chair.

After Mary and I were seated in a pair of damask-covered arm-chairs, the manservant brought our drinks.

"I was a military governor in a Zulu district," Colonel Warbur-ton explained. "And Hacker," he gestured at his servant, "was my batsman. He still serves me now."

Hacker's longtime position with the Colonel explained what had seemed mere impertinence.

Looking at the Colonel's weathered face, I was not surprised to hear he had spent much of his career in Africa. Though lines etched his face, his colour was excellent. His eyes shone with in-telligence, but were slightly clouded, perhaps by too much brandy.

As the Colonel refilled his leaded-glass, I admired a set of ivory tusks and ebony carvings of wild animals displayed on a long tres-tle table near his chair. Books on Africa and military campaigns lined the bookshelf on the wall closest to me. I made out one on Cecil Rhodes. Most prominently displayed was the title, *Shaka, King of the Zulus: Zulu Dominance in Africa.*

"You see," Colonel Warburton was saying, "I intercepted an African drum message, and I doubt there was another Englishman in the world who could have heard the sound, the drumbeats were so far away." He took a generous swallow of brandy.

"Oh, I don't doubt that, Colonel." I nodded, suspecting the li-quor embellished his story.

He continued, "I spent a good number of years studying the native customs, and I spotted the meaning right away. An uprising was planned to start throughout the whole district at noon the next day. Of course I…"

The Colonel's head rose stiffly, and he appeared to be searching the room. "There it is again, that devilish sound. I cannot stand it. Do you hear it, Doctor Watson? Mrs Watson?"

"I can hear nothing, sir," I said.

"Nor can I," Mary said, alarmed by the Colonel's sudden distress.

"Of course not. No one can hear it but me!" The Colonel pressed his fingertips to his temples as if in pain.

"Now, now, Colonel Warburton," I said, trying to calm the man, "Do not excite yourself."

"It is black magic, that's what it is!" he cried. "The powers of witchcraft have been forgotten in this country, Doctor Watson. But I know of them, and I can think of many people who may wish to employ them against me."

A knock sounded on the door of the study. The Colonel started, his eyes wide and staring as the doorknob slowly turned.

The door opened and a most regal-looking woman entered the room, followed by two Nubian servants. My gaze was drawn to the lady's face. Beautiful and black as polished ebony, it was framed by coiled and braided hair. Her attire represented the latest and most perfect taste. A feathered hat crowned her head. Her elegant dress was made of fine cloth and covered a splendid statuesque figure.

The Colonel sprang to his feet, his tense expression easing as he crossed the room. "Nada, dear. Allow me to introduce you to some friends of Ellen's. Doctor and Mrs Watson."

"I am very pleased to meet both of you." Nada spoke perfect English, betraying no accent.

The Colonel placed a hand on Nada's arm, then turned to me. "Nada's father was a Zulu chieftain, a direct descendant of the great warrior Shaka. An unexpected turn of events allowed me to save his life, and since then, he has considered me his blood brother."

Nada's dark eyes warmed as she looked at the Colonel.

"And," he continued, "when the missionaries sent Nada to England to complete her education, I insisted she spend her first few months here, under my wing. I…no!" he cried. "It is too much. I cannot bear it!"

I tried to discern what caused him such anguish, but perceived nothing. "What is it, Colonel?"

"That piercing sound again. Please say you heard it this time. Please!"

As much as I desired to help the man, I could not lie. "I did not hear a thing, sir."

"I did, and I know where that sound came from!" The Colonel rushed to the wall and grabbed a long spear with a wickedly sharp point.

Nada backed away and stood against the fireplace mantel, her eyes filled with fear.

"Put down that spear at once, Colonel Warburton!"

"John, stop him!" Mary shrieked.

"They don't have the right to kill me! I'll kill them first." Colonel Warburton was in a pitiable state, beyond hope of self control.

I heard footsteps outside the study, and so did Colonel Warburton. He drew back his arm holding the spear.

"No. No, sir," I cried. "Don't throw it. Someone is coming, you will—"

I heard Mary scream and the spear whistle through the air as someone opened the door.

The spearhead slammed into one side of the door-frame and quivered.

"Uncle! It's Ellen." White-faced, Miss Warburton stared at the spear, only inches from her head.

I drew my kerchief and mopped my brow.

"Uncle, what is going on? What is it?" Miss Warburton rushed toward him.

"The sound, like a knife in my head. It came again, Ellen. I will find where it comes from, before it finds me!" The Colonel ran wildly from the room, and Nada, followed by her servants, rushed after him.

Mary had risen from her chair, and stood quite close to me. "What a household," she whispered.

"Poor Uncle." Miss Warburton stared at us, her fingers tightly laced together. "Of course *you* heard no sound?"

"Nothing, Ellen," Mary said, with regret.

"What can we do to help him, Doctor Watson?" Miss Warburton asked me.

"It's hard to say, Miss Warburton. I'm not sure that medical help is what he needs. He seems perfectly sane and lucid except for these strange outbursts."

"But what is plaguing him? Sometimes I wonder about these Africans having free run of the house. Nada, and her two servants. I have heard things, I have seen…"

"What have you seen?" Mary asked uneasily.

"No, it is nothing."

"Miss Warburton," I said. "If you know anything that might help your uncle, you must tell me."

Turning from me, she appeared to stare at the leopard skin on the wall across the room. When she spoke, her voice trembled. "I do not want to speak ill of my uncle. But I must ask you, Doctor Watson. If my uncle fails to improve, what should be done?"

I did not want to be responsible for committing the Colonel to an asylum, nor was I sure that such a drastic measure was needed.

"Has the colonel been under the care of a family physician?" I asked.

"Yes," Miss Warburton replied. "But Doctor Stiles only thinks it some recurring malady from his days in Africa. Uncle has never had such symptoms before, and I have been close to him since he returned to England. I fear Doctor Stiles may lack the knowledge and experience that you, as a London physician, must have, Doctor Watson."

A pretty compliment indeed. But I did not want to rush to judgment. I felt quite certain now that Sherlock Holmes would take an interest in this case.

"Let me see what can be done to assist you and the Colonel, Miss Warburton," I said.

A grateful flush coloured Miss Warburton's face and her eyes were bright as she spoke. "Thank you. Thank you, Doctor Watson."

As soon as we returned to the Red Lion Inn, I posted a letter to Holmes, outlining the events that had occurred thus far. Late the next morning, the desk clerk handed me the reply from Holmes. Quickly, I led Mary into the inn's sitting room and tore the letter open.

The message was short, asking we ascertain only one important factor—did the Warburton household have a dog?

"That's a cryptic answer to my letter," I said to Mary.

"Yes, it is," she agreed. "Wise of you not to tell Ellen you were writing to Holmes. She is joining us for lunch, and might be disappointed by so little news."

"Yes," I agreed. "But I wonder, what could dogs have to do with the case?"

"I cannot imagine. Oh, here's Ellen now."

Looking up, I saw Miss Warburton enter the sitting room and walk toward us. Her chestnut hair shone in the light filtering through the white lace curtains of the room's windows, but her face appeared drawn and haggard.

Once we were seated in tapestry-covered armchairs facing a stone fireplace, Miss Warburton sighed.

"It is so kind of you to take an interest in my uncle's condition, Doctor Watson. Have you had any thoughts as to what can be done for him?"

"As a matter of fact, I wrote to Sherlock Holmes, asking for his advice in this matter."

My words appeared to startle Miss Warburton. "Surely we don't need to disturb Mr Holmes with the issue of my uncle's health," she said.

"But he's already shown interest by responding," I said. "This letter just came from him. You may read it, if you like, though I cannot see that it makes much sense, myself."

Miss Warburton's eyes widened as she read the telegram. "But that's extraordinary. I did have a little dog. He was killed a week ago. It did not occur to me to tell you about it yesterday."

"How amazing," Mary said. "How could Mr Holmes have known about it?"

"There's very little that Holmes does not know, my dear. How was your dog killed, Miss Warburton?"

"I found him on the grounds, with his head smashed in by a stone." She shuddered.

"Oh, how dreadful!" Mary said.

"Who do you think did it?" I asked.

"It might have been a poacher, and then again it might have been…"

"Your uncle?" I asked gently.

"It is possible. When he is in one of his rages, I do not think he knows what he is doing. I do not like to say it, but perhaps he should be some place where he can hurt neither himself nor anyone else." She paused a moment. "Is it necessary to trouble Mr Holmes?"

"I might not have thought so before, " I said, taking the letter back from Miss Warburton. "But this incident with your dog may be important, and Holmes's interest in the case intrigues me. Yes, I shall send Holmes a telegram at once." I rose quickly from the armchair. "Don't wait lunch for me, Mary."

The next day, I anxiously awaited a reply from Holmes. Mary insisted a walk would calm my nerves, and we ended up strolling toward the train station. In the distance, white smoke plumed and a long passenger train approached. We moved closer to watch its arrival.

When the train hissed and squealed to a stop, I approached the porter, who descended the steps of a nearby passenger car.

"I say, my dear fellow, what train is this?"

"The London train, sir. And right on time it is."

Mary and I watched the passengers step down to the platform.

"Not many people getting off," I said. "There, look! Is that Holmes with a dog on a lead?"

Indeed, it was Holmes, with a great brute of a dog. Mary and I hurried over to him and after we exchanged greetings, I drew Holmes to one side.

"I say, I'm delighted to see you, my dear fellow."

Holmes studied me with that heavy-lidded expression that so nicely veiled his keen nature.

"It occurred to me," he said, "I could be down here in the same time it would take a telegram to reach you, and a day or two in the country would be an interesting change. And, of course, Colonel Warburton's problem interests me enormously."

"But why on Earth would you bring a dog? And why not our old friend Toby?"

"Toby is getting on in years. He's not as keen as he once was. But I believe this dog may be of invaluable assistance."

When I reached a tentative hand toward the brindled beast, a deep growl rumbled from its throat, and the hackles on his neck rose.

"Do be careful, John," Mary said.

"Yes," Holmes said, "look out, old chap. I think it would be better not to pet him. I picked him up for a couple of florins on Mylan Road, and I think he would have done better to stay in London. He has a singularly unattractive nature, and he seems to have been put out by the train ride."

"Unpleasant brute," I said, pulling my hand back.

"Yes, isn't he?" Holmes replied.

"By the way, Holmes, what do you make of the case from my letters?"

"I should prefer to reserve my judgment until I have met the Colonel. However, I will offer one opinion."

"Oh, what is that?" I asked.

"To paraphrase a proverb, do not disbelieve all you do not hear."

It was late afternoon when Mary, Holmes, and I approached Chevy Grange. As we climbed the stone steps to the Colonel's doorway, the dog trailed behind Holmes on his lead.

Once again, I lifted the heavy brass knocker and rapped. When no one responded, I knocked again. "They cannot all be out," I said.

"No servants?" asked Holmes.

At his side, the dog panted heavily. "I should tie this fellow up," he said, leading the creature to a hitching post near the base of the stairs. When he fastened the dog's lead, the brindled beast snarled and bared his teeth.

"Quiet!" Holmes said sharply, and the dog subsided. Holmes moved quickly up the steps and joined us. "You might try the door," he said to me.

As I grasped the handle, the door swung open, and I stared into the dark face of Miss Nada's manservant. His unexpected presence startled me, and I could not help but remember Miss Warburton's concern about natives having the run of her uncle's house.

"Let's go in, old fellow, let's go in," Holmes said, stepping past the servant into the gloomy corridor.

Miss Nada's man seemed pleasant enough, but when we asked for the Colonel, we discovered the servant could not speak English. We called for the Colonel, Miss Warburton, and even the manservant, Hacker, but were answered by silence.

Outside the house, the dog yelped, then howled briefly, as if in pain.

"The dog!" cried Holmes. "Oh, fool that I am, I should not have left him there. Come on!"

But we were too late. The dog lay dead on the ground, one of the Colonel's spears protruding from his chest.

Mary's face paled and she turned away from the dog.

"Poor brute," I said. "This proves it, Holmes. The Colonel is mad."

"I think not, Watson. It proves that Colonel Warburton is a great deal more sane than some of the members of his household." Holmes tilted his head as if listening to some sound.

"Come with me." Quickly, Holmes guided Mary and me across the grounds toward the carriage house.

"Do you hear that, Watson?" he asked.

Mary clutched my sleeve. "What is it?"

"Shh, listen." Holmes stopped and stood still a moment.

As I strained to hear, a series of long repetitive notes reached me. "I say, Holmes, it's the same sound we heard yesterday."

"Yes," he said. "And what's more, it's coming from the carriage house. Come on, but quietly."

The sound of voices chanting and the beating of drums grew louder. I might not admit it, but I was rather proud of Mary. Instead of exhibiting fear, her face glowed with eagerness and excitement.

"Here," Holmes said quietly. "We can see through this window."

I peered through the dusty glass. "Nada, and her servant woman," I whispered.

As I watched, the servant beat two small drums, her head thrown back in some emotion I couldn't fathom. Feather bracelets adorned her arms and quivered in the glow of an oil lantern. Both she and Nada chanted, but Nada's behaviour was far more restrained.

"Who's that man with her?" Holmes asked.

"Colonel Warburton." I squinted to get a better look. "No, it isn't. It's that servant fellow, Hacker. What the devil is he doing in there?" Hacker sat on a short wooden barrel, his hands folded as if in prayer, his eyes downcast.

"It appears he and Miss Nada are practicing some form of mysticism," Holmes replied quietly.

"Extraordinary," Mary whispered, her eyes shining.

"The Colonel was right," I said. "It's black magic. Let's go in and catch them at it."

"No," replied Holmes. "Stay quiet. We'll talk to them soon enough. At the moment, I feel it is much more urgent we find Colonel Warburton. Come on."

When we skirted the stand of trees closer to the house, we found the Colonel pacing up and down in front of the stone steps with Miss Warburton. As I watched, he threw a desperate look at the dead dog.

I whispered to Holmes, "The Colonel and his niece, Miss Warburton. We shouldn't have left him alone with her. He's dangerous."

"Apart from the fact that we were unaware of their whereabouts, I do not believe Miss Warburton is in danger, Watson," Holmes said.

The Colonel caught sight of us, and with Miss Warburton close behind, he hurried toward us.

"Sherlock Holmes, eh?" he said. "I suppose you think I killed your wretched dog?" His hands trembled violently as he spoke. "Well, I might have done it. When I hear that dreadful sound, something seems to snap in my brain. I might have killed the dog. Why doesn't your doctor friend certify me as insane? Send me where I belong, before I do any worse damage!"

With a wail, the Colonel ran from us and disappeared into the house.

"How wonderful that you have come, Mr Holmes," Miss Warburton said. "My poor uncle. Is there anything you can do for him?"

"I will certainly try, Miss Warburton." Turning to me, he said, "Watson, old fellow, we should follow the Colonel and find him a brandy. I'm afraid he has quite an ordeal before him."

"He could use something to steady his nerves," I replied. "But what do you mean by *ordeal*?"

"In good time, Watson," he said.

As we entered the hall, Miss Warburton said she would bring brandy from the library. When she started to turn away, Holmes spoke to her.

"One moment, Miss Warburton. Could you tell me where you were when my dog was killed?"

"Down in the greenhouse," she replied without hesitation. "As soon as I heard the animal, I ran to the house. Such a terrible thing. And poor Uncle, I should pour him that drink." She hurried off on her errand.

"Mr Holmes," Mary said, "you are going to be able to help the Colonel, aren't you?"

"I'm convinced of it, Mrs Watson. But now that the dog is dead...I must obtain another one before I can proceed further with the case." Holmes turned to me speaking briskly. "Watson, see that the Colonel receives a *generous* dose of brandy, will you?"

"Yes, of course," I replied.

The words were hardly out of my mouth when Holmes turned and dashed away down the hall.

"But where are you going?" I called after him.

"I must find a witness." And with that, he was gone.

Outside the Colonel's bedroom, Miss Warburton handed me a large snifter of brandy. With Hacker's assistance, I soon had Colonel Warburton propped against several pillows at the head of his bed. His hands trembled as he lifted the liquor to his lips, but by the time he found the bottom of his glass, he had regained his self control.

"I do not know what comes over me," he said. "I do hope Mr Holmes can make sense of this miserable affair."

Hacker leaned over and straightened a stray pillow next to the Colonel. "There now, Colonel. No doubt it will be sorted out soon enough. Can I get you another brandy, sir?"

I did not trust this Hacker. He was just as likely to provide more black incantations like those I'd witnessed in the carriage house.

My thoughts were interrupted by Holmes calling me from the hall below. When I reached the staircase, I was astonished to see Holmes at the foot of the steps with a handsome black-and-tan foxhound. I hurried down to them.

"Watson," he said. "I need you to gather the household in the study."

"I'll get them," I said. "But where did you find that dog?"

"The huntsman for the Taplow Hunt resides just down the road. He lent me this dog for a half-crown. A beauty, isn't he? His name is Digby."

"You are not going to expose him to any danger are you?" Surely, two dead dogs were enough.

"None, Watson, otherwise I shouldn't have borrowed him. I'm convinced Digby can provide us with a clue about Colonel Warburton's affliction."

Holmes stood by the trestle table that displayed the ivory tusks and carved figures. His eyes held a glint I immediately recognized. Mary sat close to me on a settee as I watched the anxious faces of the residents of Chevy Grange.

Miss Nada, on a horsehair sofa, remained stiff and formal as if her regal upbringing alone would maintain her composure. Her manservant and the woman who had beaten the drums stood by the sofa, watching over their mistress.

Hacker appeared scornful of the entire event. He stood behind the Colonel's armchair with his lip slightly curled. Colonel Warburton grasped his brandy glass, a slight tremble visible in his hands. Was he afraid of what Holmes might uncover?

"Let me begin," Holmes said, studying the room's occupants. "Now, you are all here, the Colonel, Miss Warburton, Miss Nada, her two servants, Hacker, and the dog Digby. I propose to conduct an experiment. Before I proceed, I should like to point out the chronology of the events in this case. First, Miss Nada arrived here in England and took up residence at Chevy Grange."

"Mr Holmes," Nada protested, rising from the sofa, "you are not suggesting that I—"

"Allow me to finish, Miss Nada." Holmes's words were swift and certain.

Miss Nada settled back with a defiant look, as Holmes continued.

"As I said, first Miss Nada arrived here. Second, the Colonel first heard the mysterious, piercing noise. Third, your dog was killed, Miss Warburton. Fourth, the painful noise set in with a vengeance."

He paused, then his glance settled on the Warburtons.

"Colonel Warburton and Miss Warburton, doesn't that pattern suggest something to you?"

"No, I cannot say that it does, Mr Holmes," Miss Warburton said.

"What are you driving at?" the Colonel asked gruffly.

"Holmes," I said. "I wish you would be more specific."

"Then I will. I shall conduct my experiment. Watson, I want you to watch Colonel Warburton and the dog, Digby. Excuse me," Holmes said and turned away so we could only see his back. "Now!"

The Colonel clapped his hands over both ears. "Oh, please, God. Not again!" The Colonel gave a shriek of pain just as the foxhound lifted his head and howled.

"The dog!" Wide-eyed, his hands dropping to his lap, the Colonel stared at Digby. "He heard it, too!"

"Indeed," I said, rising to my feet. "Holmes, I am quite in the dark. What does it mean?"

"It is simplicity itself," Holmes replied, whirling to face us. He held a small wooden object in his hand.

"This whistle is the answer to the mystery. The sound made by this cunning instrument is above the normal range of pitch. You see, the Colonel is hypersensitive to certain sounds."

Miss Warburton clutched at the arms of her chair. "Then Uncle is not mad! Thank God!"

"But," I said, "the dog heard it."

Holmes smiled. "Perhaps I should have said above the normal *human* range of pitch."

"Has someone deliberately been trying to drive the Colonel mad?" Mary asked.

"Of course, Mary," I said. "That's why the dogs were murdered! Whoever it was knew a dog would give the game away."

Miss Warburton rose stiffly from her chair and stared at Nada. "And it's not hard to guess who that someone is. Nada, this started when *you* came here. Is this your gratitude for the Colonel's kindness? Endangering his sanity with your evil black magic?"

"That is not true!" Nada said.

Holmes held up a hand. "One moment, Miss Warburton. Please, you must calm yourself."

Reluctantly, Miss Warburton took her seat again.

"Miss Nada," Holmes continued. "Doctor Watson and I watched you in the carriage house some half-hour ago with Hacker and your woman servant. Were you engaged in practicing a form of black magic?"

"No, Mr Holmes," she responded in her soft voice. "I was praying to my old gods to save the Colonel's sanity."

"And what were you doing there, Hacker?" I asked. "Don't tell me you were praying to the old gods, too?"

"No. I used to be a chapel-going man." A flush of embarrassment coloured Hacker's cheeks. "So...so, I don't know. There's no harm in trying something new, I always say."

"In any case, why would Miss Nada want to persecute the Colonel?" asked Holmes.

"Perhaps it's some form of tribal revenge," Miss Warburton said, glaring at Nada.

"That's ridiculous, Ellen," said Colonel Warburton. "Her father made me his blood brother."

"Exactly, sir." Holmes was thoroughly enjoying the moment. "No," he said, "it should be obvious who had a motive for making the Colonel appear mad. His *niece*—who also happens to be his only heir."

"You don't mean that," cried Mary.

"But you will remember Miss Warburton has studied physics and so would know about supersonic research. Possibly she feared the Colonel might leave his estate to Miss Nada and so wished him to appear insane, and thereby invalidate any new will."

Holmes's hard stare fastened on Miss Warburton. "In any case, I found this whistle in a drawer in *your* room, Miss Warburton."

The blood drained from Miss Warburton's face, and her fingers looked clawlike as they grasped the chair arms.

The Colonel rose. "Ellen! Ellen how could you?"

"I did it for your sake, to save you from Nada," Miss Warburton shouted. "She's just an adventuress, only you won't see it." Miss Warburton collapsed in her chair and burst into tears.

"My God!" Mary whispered to me. "And she killed her own little dog."

"Colonel Warburton," said Holmes. "What action do you wish me to take regarding your niece?"

"My *niece*?" The Colonel's face hardened as he turned from Miss Warburton and moved next to Nada. "I have no niece, Mr Holmes. Come, Nada, my dear."

Miss Warburton shrank deeper into her chair as, arm in arm, Colonel Warburton and Miss Nada left the room.

✗

NOTE: *this story is very loosely based on a radio play by Denis Greene and Anthony Boucher of the same title.*

COUNTRY COOKING

by John M. Floyd

There were twelve ladies knitting in the library conference room when Sheriff Lucy Valentine cracked the door and eased her head inside. She was not at all surprised to see that her mother, retired schoolteacher Fran Valentine, was doing most of the talking.

"Mother?" she said. "Can I have a minute?"

It was no more than a loud whisper, but every woman in the room stopped knitting and swiveled to look at the door. Lucy did an embarrassed little finger-wave and focused again on her mom, who gave the other ladies an apologetic look and an eyeroll, rose from her chair, and stomped across the room.

"What is it?" she said.

Lucy motioned to her and backed out into the hallway. Fran followed.

When the two of them were alone Lucy opened her mouth to speak and then paused, studying the huge wad of woolen fabric in her mother's hands. "What are you making? A blanket?"

"A sweater. What do you want?—I'm busy."

Lucy felt her face heat up. "I'm busy too, Mother. I happen to be trying to catch a fugitive."

"Here in the library?"

She sighed. "No, not here. I just found out Billy Ray Cobb escaped from prison this morning."

"Billy Ray?"

"And stole a car."

Fran frowned and shook her head. "Can't say I'm surprised. He's an even bigger idiot than his daddy was. But what does Billy Ray Cobb have to do with me?"

"You know his mother, don't you? Wilma?"

"We knew each other in school. She cooks at one of those greasy spoons out on the highway. Why?"

"I need you to call her, that's why. Ask her if she's heard from Billy Ray today."

Fran seemed to give that some thought. "You're right, she might be able to help. Wilma's told me she loves him—he is her son, after all—but deep down, I think she knows he belongs in jail."

"So you'll phone her?"

"Sure. We're almost done here anyway."

Lucy checked her watch. "Call me if you find out something, okay? I need to get back to the office."

"Anything else?" Fran asked. Lucy tried to keep from smiling; grumpy and stubborn as Fran Valentine was, she loved police work. She especially loved interfering in police work, which was usually the case—but she also like being asked to help.

"I'll keep you updated." Lucy hesitated, looking again at how much material her mother was holding. *Sweater?* she thought. "That's not intended for me, is it?"

Fran looked down at her project. "It's for my neighbor. Why?"

"Is your neighbor Andre the Giant?"

"Maybe you better stick to crimefighting," Fran said, "and leave the knitting to me."

An hour later Sheriff Valentine's office phone rang. She answered it, listened a moment, made a quick reply, hung up, and turned to her deputy, Ed Malone. "That was my mother. We got a break."

She dug a map out of a drawer and spread it out on her desktop. Malone joined her. "What kind of break?" he asked.

"Wilma Cobb was all upset. Said her son called her a while ago. He's headed in this direction."

"Why? A family visit?"

"No, Mother said he told his ma he's on his way to fetch the ten grand he stole from that bank a year ago. Said it's buried at the old Yeager farm."

"Fran got Ms. Cobb to tell her this?"

"Mother can get almost anyone to tell her anything. Do you know where it is—the Yeager place?"

Malone leaned over, squinted, and pointed to a spot on the map. "Right about there. A mile or so off the highway." He looked up at Lucy. "What else did she find out?"

"Well, Billy Ray told Wilma the money's hidden under the kitchen floorboards, three feet behind the cookstove."

Malone frowned. "I don't get it. Why would Billy Ray tell her all that?"

Lucy stood up and rubbed her eyes. "He said he wants her to know where to find it in case he's caught before he makes it that far." She picked up her hat and car keys. "Come on—we'll call for backup on the way."

"What about Fran?"

"Are you kidding? Believe me, she'll be there too. Probably before we are."

The two of them arrived at the scene only minutes behind four state cops in two cruisers and—sure enough—Fran Valentine. Their cars were parked on a gravel side-road two hundred yards west of the abandoned Yeager place, and they were all crouched like bandits in the thick woods a hundred yards closer in. From that position, they could see the huge main house and a smaller building out back. The farm, Lucy knew, had been a working plantation in the early- to mid-1800s, and had never been modernized. For a time it had even been a tourist attraction. Now it was just another forgotten cluster of buildings in disrepair, with weeds and broomsedge three feet high surrounding it in all directions.

"I like your hat," Deputy Malone said to Fran. She was wearing aviator sunglasses and an Atlanta Braves baseball cap turned backwards. She grinned at him like a little kid.

Lucy waded past them into the assembled group. "What do you think?" she asked the oldest-looking of the men.

"We saw a car parked in the trees way over there," he said, pointing east. "Must be the one he stole—who else would be out here?"

All of them except Fran took a moment to check their weapons, and one of the state troopers made a cell phone call, probably a situation report. After a quick and grim-faced strategy session, Ed Malone was dispatched to the area where the car had been spotted, to cut off any possible road escape, and the four patrolmen sprinted across the field to the house. They edged along the front wall, drew their guns, and—at a signal from their leader—crept inside the building's two open doors. The sheriff and her mother had been told to stay put, in order to watch and report in. Lucy found herself wondering if it was because they were the only two women. She hoped not, but when dealing with state cops in the rural South one never knew for sure.

Suddenly Fran gasped. "I just thought of something," she said. She rose to her feet and, without another word, took off running toward the farm.

"Mother? Wait a minute!"

Lucy had no choice but to follow her. A minute later they were standing outside the door of the small building behind the main house, sweating and breathing hard. Thorns had ripped one of the legs of Lucy's uniform from knee to ankle. "What the hell do you think you're doing?" she blurted.

"I'm doing what the others should've done," Fran said. "Billy Ray's not over there in the big house. He never was."

"Then where is he?"

"He's in here," Fran whispered, nodding at the door.

"What?!"

Fran pointed to Lucy's holstered revolver. "Get that out and get it ready."

Lucy drew the pistol. "It's ready."

"Just make sure you don't shoot *me* with it."

Fran held up one finger, then two, then three—and she and Sheriff Valentine surged together through the door. And sure enough, there stood Billy Ray Cobb, dirty from head to toe, half in and half out of a hole in the wooden floor near an old stove. In his hands were a shovel and a filthy canvas bank bag and on his face was the most surprised expression Lucy had ever seen. "Freeze!" she shouted—something she had always wanted to say—and leveled her gun at an already frozen Billy Ray.

She held her pistol on him while Fran summoned the troops, and five minutes later the hapless fugitive was handcuffed and arrested and escorted through the weeds and brambles toward the waiting patrol cars. Deputy Malone followed the parade, carrying the bag of stolen cash.

Lucy and Fran stood outside the small house, watching. Lucy had taken her hat off; her hair was sticking out in every direction. "I can't believe it," she said finally.

"What can't you believe?"

"How'd you know Billy Ray wasn't in the main house? Are you a mind reader?"

"No," Fran said, smiling. "I'm a history reader."

"What do you mean?"

"I should've thought of it earlier. Plantation homes in the nineteenth century never had their cookstoves in the main residence. The kitchen was always in a separate building."

Lucy blinked. "You're kidding."

"It's a fact. There was too much danger of fire to do otherwise."

Lucy was quiet a moment, watching her mother watch the others trudge away across the weed-choked field. Fran had turned her ball cap around the right way, but she still looked ridiculous standing there in the sun, in the cap and sunglasses and a lime-green pant suit.

"That was good work, Mother," Lucy said.

Fran shrugged. "They'd have caught him anyway. Especially since Malone was out there watching the getaway car."

"But this way nobody got hurt." For a moment Lucy pictured a shootout between her deputy and Billy Ray, and shivered. "That was clever thinking."

"Elementary, my dear sheriff," Fran said. She turned then to look hard at her daughter. "By the way, one of those troopers was giving you the eye. And I didn't see any wedding ring."

"I didn't see anybody giving me the eye." Lucy put her hat back on, tucked her torn trouser-leg into her boot, and started walking toward the cars. "Maybe you better stick to knitting," she said, "and leave the husband-hunting to me."

Fran snorted and followed her. "That'd be two lost causes."

"I thought you liked knitting," Lucy said, over her shoulder.

"I'm having second thoughts." Fran looked up at the cloudless sky and adjusted her sunglasses as they walked. "You really think the sweater's too big?"

"The one you showed me, that you're making?"

"Right."

"Yeah, it's too big."

Fran thought that over and nodded. "Maybe I better stick to crimefighting," she said.

✗

FOOT PATROL

by Laird Long

Officers George Hutchins and Tracy Garza were on routine night foot patrol near the waterfront when a man suddenly staggered out of the mouth of an alley and bumped into them.

"Officers! Police officers! Thank goodness!" he gushed. "I've been robbed! I was just robbed!"

Garza steadied the swaying man, then wrinkled her nose. "Have you been drinking, sir?"

"Yes! I've been drinking! But I was just robbed!"

"What happened?" Hutchins asked.

"Well, like I told your partner, I had a few at the Crown and Anchor. Then I left, and walked down to the ATM at the bank branch over there." He waved vaguely behind him. "I withdrew five hundred dollars. In twenties. That's…"

"Twenty-five twenties," Garza said helpfully.

"Right! And I rolled them like I do—into a big roll held tight together with an elastic band. Stuffed it into my pants's pocket. And then, when I was walking down this alley—not more than a minute ago!—I felt a hand reach into my pocket. I grabbed at the hand, and someone pushed me down, made off with my roll!"

"Just now?"

"Just…Yes! Now!"

Hutchins gestured at his patrol partner, and Officer Garza took off running up the alley.

"You stay right here, sir," Hutchins said, guiding the man backwards until he was propped up against the brick wall of a store, "while we check it out."

Hutchins jogged up the alley, out the other side. He was the senior officer, almost thirty years Garza's senior, so he let her handle the fast-pursuits. It was good experience for a rookie.

He'd trotted two blocks along the darkened city sidewalk when he heard a shout, saw someone waving way up ahead. He caught up with his partner another two blocks over.

Garza had stopped a woman for questioning—a tall, lean, blond woman wearing a tight, pink crop-top and tight, white short-shorts, a pair of white sneakers with pink shoelaces.

"This is Britney Womack, isn't it, George?" Officer Garza asked her partner. "Known drunk-roller with an arrest record as long as her arms?"

"You were listening and watching at the briefing this morning, Tracy—about all the muggings in this area lately, and the possible suspects. Nice work."

Hutchins knew Britney Womack from more than just her mug-shot, however; from on-the-job contact. "Out jogging at this late hour, Britney? In this neighborhood?"

"There's no law against it, is there, Officer Hutchins?" the woman responded politely. "I like to keep in shape. And it's such a beautiful warm night."

"Uh-huh. And you wouldn't know anything about a roll of cash that was just lifted off a man in an alley near here a few minutes ago, would you?"

Womack smiled. "Do you see a roll of cash anywhere on me?"

The two officers studied the woman's skimpy, skin-tight exercise outfit, didn't see anything but the normal bulges.

"We could search you," Garza stated.

"If you have probable cause," Womack countered.

Hutchins said, "Well, I guess it was just a coincidence that you happened to be in the same area when this mugging went down." He was looking at the woman's feet, her bright white sneakers with the pink laces tied up in neat bows. "Okay, Britney, take a walk."

Garza started to protest, but Hutchins held up his hand. "Go on, Britney," he said. "Walk."

The woman hesitated. Then she slowly turned, started walking away down the sidewalk, limping slightly on her right.

Hutchins commented, "I'd say we have a probable cause for a body search now, wouldn't you, Officer Garza?"

Garza blinked, then grinned. She ran over to Womack and took hold of the woman's arm.

"She's got the money hidden in her sneaker," Officer Garza stated. "How did you know for sure, George?"

"Just trained observation from years of experience," Officer Hutchins replied modestly. "You see," he pointed, "the shoelace bow on Britney's right sneaker is smaller than the one on her left sneaker, indicating she has something in that shoe which is pushing her foot up higher. Like a hidden roll of stolen cash."

Garza nodded. "Time to do the *perp walk*, Britney. Back to the stationhouse."

THE KILLING OF GENERAL PATTON

by William E. Chambers

My dreams have been haunted by the *accident* intermittently since December of 1945 although each year they occur less frequently than the year before.

Sometimes I wake up feeling lost and anguished, sometimes feeling peace, occasionally even elation that the ordeal's behind me. The Nazi camp or *Stalag* where I served my imprisonment as guest of the Third Reich was liberated during an intense battle in which barbed wire fences were crushed under the treads of American tanks behind which flowed a stream of infantrymen triggering bayoneted M1's and blazing Thompson submachine guns. Between the first and second waves of infantry stood a man in the rear of a top down Jeep firing white handled Colt revolvers at Nazi soldiers in desperate retreat. This near surreal personage who never flinched as bullets whizzed around him bore the markings of a General on his helmet. That was my first glimpse of George S. Patton.

Disbelieving my own eyes I watched this spectral figure, defiantly mocking an enemy most of the world dreaded, shrink into drizzled fog and clouds of gun smoke then vanish before the wave of foot soldiers advancing behind him. The rest of the afternoon was a cacophony of clatter: bursting grenades; the rattle of the Thompson; and the distinct single shot snap of the M1 mingled with cries, moans, and curses—followed by an abrupt and utter silence right after nightfall. Staring into the darkness through my barred window I inhaled the acrid fumes of battle and felt as though the God of War had ordered an immediate ceasefire.

I lay in my bunk staring up at nothing and tuning out the fear and hope distinguished in the chatter of my fellow POW's. I had learned through the past eight months to expect only the worst and now I refused to drop my psychological guard. Hopes cannot be dashed if you have none. Somehow while that phrase kept circling my mind I dropped off to sleep. When I sat up it was with fists cocked and teeth clenched. I didn't recognize the sounds coming from my throat. A rugged but kindly face addressed me, "Easy soldier."

My eyelids fluttered like the wings of a horsefly. My mouth moved but no words were formed. The tall muscular man under the general's helmet turned to a sergeant and said, "Give this man some water."

"Yes sir."

My hands shook so as the sergeant pressed the canteen into them that he placed his palms against my wrists and brought the spout up to my lips. At first the water seemed to boil in my throat then a refreshing coolness overcame my first swallow. When the canteen was drained I felt steadier and handed it back. The general gently rubbed my shoulder and said, "You're safe now, son…"

✗   ✗   ✗   ✗

A little more than a week ago a phone call brought those dreams back full force and I've awakened every morning for the last week only lost and anguished—elation denied. The voice on the other end of the line spoke fluent English, no trace of an accent at all, "Mr. Burton Wells?"

"Yes. Who's calling?"

"Vitali Darahofsky."

"That's absurd…" A chill ran through me. "I read his obituary."

"It was only printed in the Russian newspapers, but then again you do read and speak Russian, don't you?"

"I—uh," Very few people knew that. This caller caught me off guard. I should have said nothing. "Who—uh—who is this really? And what do you want?"

"It's difficult to explain over the phone. I'm on assignment in Ukraine at the moment but I should be finished anytime now. Then I'm coming to the States and I'd like to pay you a visit in your Greenwich Village brownstone. I must go now."

"A visit! Hold on now. I want to know—"

The phone went dead. I inserted it into the cradle, stood up and walked over to my living room bay window and looked down at lovers, gay and straight, arm in arm or holding hands, enjoying the spring night as my wife Megan and I first did sixty years ago. Then I turned and looked up at the oil portrait of a flaming haired, green eyed beauty in a spotless wedding dress that hung high up over the fireplace. She's gone over ten years now but dwells in my memory every day.

My living room is a hodgepodge of overstuffed armchairs, a sofa, end tables, and a coffee and cream oval throw rug atop a blond hardwood floor. A small, portable bar adorns one corner of the room. A vintage German Luger removed by me from the dead body of a German soldier that I killed hangs by the trigger guard under my wife's portrait above the fireplace mantel. Before I was captured I buried that pistol beneath an outsized boulder and retrieved it after my liberation. When I showed it to General Patton he said, "Son, you want this gun to go home I'll see that it gets there. After what you've sacrificed for your country you certainly deserve it."

"Thank you, sir. I'll include an explanation to my father."

"Do that. He should be proud of you."

I wrote the letter and gave it to the general who somehow avoided the wartime censors. The package arrived intact at my parent's home through the regular US Mail. My two purple hearts and one Silver Star hang in a frame next to the weapon. Another great token of honor, the Order of Lenin, is buried inconspicuously at the back bottom of my wall safe behind Megan's picture. It was presented to me in January of 1946 by the Soviet Ambassador to the United Nations, Andrei Gromyko, at a midnight ceremony in his Sutton Place apartment. I was cautioned that this must remain a secret and therefore Stalin ordered that no written documentation be included. If ever the medal should be discovered, the Soviets would dismiss it as a fake. Now, however, I had the feeling that its secrecy might be endangered.

I was still pondering this situation when the chiming of the doorbell shattered my uneasy reverie. I buzzed back then walked into the brightly lit hall. The young man below sported a wide brimmed fedora hat, aviator eyeglasses, and a sweatshirt bearing Shakespeare's face. He wore skinny legged black jeans. Real Hipster, I thought before saying, "Can I help you?"

"Winding down jetlag, sir, long trip from Ukraine…"

"Ukraine? You're…uh…my recent caller…"

"Vitali. Can we speak in private?"

"I live alone."

"I know that." His faux grin failed to mask the boldness of his tone. "May I come up?"

"Come up."

"Thank you, sir." He bounded up the long staircase two steps at a time then extended his hand. "Sure could use a drink. Got vodka?"

Though offended by his demeanor, I clasped his hand and read his shirt. The image of Shakespeare holding two foaming mugs with the caption, *Two beers or not two beers. That is the question.*" was emblazoned in yellow across the otherwise dark material. At least my intruder had a sense of humor. At close range he looked a little older than the average twenty-something hipster. I said, "Come in. I've got vodka."

Vitali glanced approvingly all around the room and stopped to admire Megan's portrait while I walked over to the rolling bar. "Straight up or rocks," I asked.

"Straight up would be fine."

Saying nothing more, he shifted his attention to the Luger and the medals. When I handed him the oversized tumbler he noted, "You make a powerful drink."

"Well, you're a Russian, right?"

"Do I look like a Russian?"

"In that getup you look like central casting."

This grin seemed more sincere than that first smile down the hall. He chuckled before answering, "Grandpa was in the NKVD which morphed eventually into the KGB. He told me to always fit in wherever I go. And this is 'The Village,' right?"

I didn't bother to answer.

Vitali motioned with his glass. "Aren't you going to join me?"

"Gave it up when I turned eighty. Keep stuff around for friends and…uh…others. Which one are you?"

"Lovely portrait of your wife. Medals are impressive, too."

"Can't answer the question?"

Vitali raised his drink hand up, tilted the fedora back with his thumb and actually rolled the tumbler across his forehead before answering, "Consider me a business colleague."

As he lowered the glass I said, "With a flair for the dramatic."

"Acting's as necessary as food for survival, Mr. Wells. Convincingly presenting who you want to appear to be rather than whom you truly are is a prerequisite for success—even for survival. As you well know…"

I motioned to one of the sofas, "Sit down."

He obliged, took a deep swallow and wiggled his empty glass in the air. I fetched him another then dropped back into one of the armchairs while asking, "What is the purpose of this visit?"

"Well, since you were a friend of my grandfather's—a confidante even when he was your party boss—I thought I would discuss the good old days with you, or as they now say, discuss happenings 'back in the day.'"

"Happenings." I began to feel queasy. "What sort of happenings?"

Vitali removed his hat, dropped it on his knee and reworked the tumbler forehead act. Above his face, brown hair was thinning. Finally he answered, "There are many things to talk about. Perhaps we'll start with the wood bullet."

My mouth was closed but I felt like I swallowed something cold. "Wood—wood bullets…"

"Clever things those wood bullets," Vitali's voice took on a sing-song quality, "especially if they are made to look something like the cork in a child's popgun. Then no one even knows it's a bullet. 'Course in this day and age children have computer guns so they don't need—they don't even know about popguns at all. And the advantage to wood is it burns up in fires. It can be launched from a relatively noiseless air gun. It splinters on impact causing major bodily damage while literally disappearing to shreds—"

I interrupted in a very calm tone. Much like the voice level I employed before shooting that Nazi soldier when his Luger jammed. Rather than surrender at my urging he attempted to adjust the weapon, so I fired my M1. Now that self-protective killing urge was coming back to me. "Why don't you cut the bullshit."

"Testy…testy… No need for vulgarity. Fact is you recuperated fast from your ordeal in the prison camp despite the meager meals doled out by your captors. Your youth—only nineteen—probably helped. The younger the body, the stronger the body, the quicker the recovery, especially when you always kept in shape, am I right?"

I didn't answer.

"Do you still exercise regularly?"

"Exercise?"

"Dynamic Tension, the lessons you learned from the Charles Atlas course your father ordered through a coupon in one of your comic books as a birthday gift when you were twelve. The same exercises you tried to teach your army comrades. Still doing them?"

"Matter of fact," Vitali was making it clear he knew me inside out, "I am."

"You look great. And I know for a fact that most of the veterans of your era are either feeble or dead. When my grandfather went he was a mere shell of the man he—"

Again I spoke evenly. "As I said before—"

"Cut the bullshit!" He placed his empty glass on an end table then raised outstretched palms in an imitation of supplication. "Forgive me. I do get carried away."

Instinctively my eyes traveled toward the Luger. His glance bounced from me to the weapon and back. Then he grinned and said, "Not a good idea. You have too much to lose if anything happens to me. Now General Patton had a habit of reviewing the records of all the men he commanded and all the ones he liberated. If anything, he was thorough. That's why he was labeled a Fascist and a Nazi for slapping a soldier he believed was a slacker. I understand he barely flicked the man's face with his gloves but it made good press.

"Well, he reviewed your case too, PFC Wells. And he liked what he found. You finished high school at seventeen and signed up for the army on your eighteenth birthday. You excelled as an infantryman and then as a sniper. You tried to keep your fellow soldiers's morale up even though you later confessed to Patton that there were times when you really believed all was lost. Your compatriots spoke so highly of your wartime exploits that he commended you for a Silver Star, which you were awarded. And he took you under his wing as an aide-de-camp to him personally." Vitali let his voice drop to a stage whisper then drift off. "What he didn't know…"

When I didn't respond he gestured with the empty tumbler. This time I told him, "Get it yourself. You know where the bar is."

Vitali propped his hat on the back of his head then stood up and threw me a false whisper. "What he didn't know was that you morally opposed the war until Hitler double crossed Stalin. Shame… shame… That's when you insisted on joining up to fight the Germans."

While he headed to the bar with his back to me I thought of making a play for the Luger. I adjusted it to work properly back in my army days and kept it loaded and handy when home alone, which is most of the time, in the event of unwanted intruders. But I thought better of the weapon idea because in good shape or not, you slow down in your eighties. And if I did get the drop on him, what then? Without knowing what his game is I had no idea which authorities to contact or what the consequences of his sudden appearance in my life might mean for me or my loved ones. So I sat back and waited until he returned with another drink. Maybe alcohol saturation would loosen his tongue.

I noticed his eyes starting to shine beneath the Aviator glasses. The vodka was doing its work. When he took his seat I asked, "Are you comfortable?"

"I make a good living."

My face involuntarily twitched from annoyance. "What?"

"It's a joke. This businessman gets hit by a car. The ambulance attendant props him up and asks—"

"I'm not in the mood for jokes. Besides, it's getting late. At my age I don't know how much time I have left on this planet. Could we get to the point before my time is up?"

"Surly...surly..." He shook his head and gulped the drink, then continued, "Anyhow the general thought so much of you he let you be his gofer and chauffeur and such. You were even supposed to be with him the day he and his chief-of-staff Major Hobart R. Gay, known as "Hap," went hunting pheasants in the German countryside outside Mannheim, but you begged off for a liaison with a non-existent *fraulein*. Patton was used to getting what he wanted but that was one motive he clearly understood would boost the morale of troops like you, thus he gave his blessing and assigned a technical sergeant named Woodring to drive in your place. So he went off on his pheasant hunt and you went off on a hunt of another kind. Correct so far?"

"You talk. I'll listen."

"Patton hated all totalitarian dictatorships and he was stating publicly that we should attack the Russian Communists before they could rebuild their armed forces. That attitude put him on Stalin's death list. You were a marksman. Patton's accident was a setup. A paid German civilian stepped in front of a truck driven by one Sergeant Thompson, who swerved to avoid an accident and hit Patton's Cadillac. That's when you fired the first shot of the Cold War, striking the general in the neck and damaging his spinal cord. The wood bullet broke up, making his wound harder for the doctors to treat. Had the road been clear of vehicles, a back-up car driven by communists would have plowed into Patton's auto. The idea was not to start a world-wide commotion by an obvious assassination but to make his death seem like an accident. A Russian soldier was also dispatched from the Red Army to back you up in case something went wrong, but he never did his job and never came back to his barracks. Apparently he was a deserter who crossed over to the enemy. Grandpa was the Commissar in charge of this operation and he believed this deserter told the Americans about the assassination plan, but that the OSS covered it up for political reasons.

"My grandfather told me that you secretly became a communist at the age of sixteen after meeting that Irish-American firebrand that you eventually married. Her grandfather had been wounded in the march on Washington staged by World War I vets who felt they were cheated out of the bonuses originally promised them by the government. The man who allegedly ordered the shooting was none other than the esteemed Douglas MacArthur. That may be fact or fiction, but the general certainly had a hand in removing the marchers.

"Raised blue collar class on Manhattan's lower East Side, your girlfriend—later wife—rebelled against the forces of what she considered *corrupted* capitalism and the rigid sexual strictures of the Catholic Church. Communism's free love dogma was far more appealing to her lusty nature and she quickly seduced you after meeting you at a ball thrown by the Teamsters. Her father worked with your father—both drivers for the same trucking outfit. Soon you fell in love and joined the party too. Correct?"

"Why ask. You seem to know more about me than I know about myself."

"Never hurts to reaffirm a fact. Anyhow my point is this. I need money. You have money. You also have secrets. And I know them. You pay me money. I keep my mouth shut. Your daughter Tara is a highly regarded heart surgeon in San Francisco. Her husband is a partner in a respected law firm. Your granddaughter—also

Tara—is an accomplished stage actress here in New York City. Family shame is the last thing you need to bring down upon them. Am I right?"

"You're right. How did you gather all these minute details about…uh…everything?"

"I told you. Grandpa was KGB and while in Germany, your boss."

"KGB agents were very tight lipped people."

"Toward the end the old man was losing it. He loved to babble, especially to me. I was his favorite. After the battle of Leningrad he was decorated by Stalin himself. Order of Lenin, something you know all about. A few years later came the purges. Being a dedicated communist he was forced to arrest and sometimes execute men he knew were Soviet loyalists. Grandpa was protected from Stalin's paranoid imaginings by his boyhood companion and communist mentor—the man who eventually succeeded Stalin as prime minister—Nikita Khrushchev. Under Khrushchev's management Grandpa rose in rank and power. But the duplicity of Soviet politics convinced him to insure his own survival with an alternate plan. He began taking photos of top secret KGB files in case he felt the need to defect to the west. This would give him something to barter with in exchange for asylum for himself and his family. As a high ranking Soviet agent he was allowed a small business on the side, so to speak, and he chose a farm. He hid these documents in camouflaged containers down a dried-up well on this property.

"A socialist at heart, he never betrayed his government but he kept taking pictures throughout the Cold War as survival insurance. He continued this policy right up to the disintegration of the Soviet Empire. When his whole belief system collapsed around him he retired to the farm, broken in mind and spirit. His son, my father, made a decent living in the black market during the last days of the USSR and used his savings to go into business after the hammer and sickle fell. But there's no *real* money to be made in Russia today unless you're in the pocket of Vladimir Putin. However there's plenty of opportunity in the good ol' USA. You've embraced capitalism, I see, and you've done very well too. What made you see the light?"

"When the handwriting is on the wall you don't ignore it. I opened up a deli, expanded to a supermarket, and built up a chain. My wife was a perpetual cigarette smoker and she died of cancer. Once my daughter was out of the house, I sold all the supermarkets."

"Very cool."

"How much do you want?"

"I'm not greedy."

"How much?"

"Compared to what you have, not much."

Not bothering to conceal my impatience, I heaved a sigh, "How much?"

"One million dollars. In fifties. They're easier to break than hundreds."

"That's twenty thousand bills."

"You're a human calculator."

"For all the accusations you made tonight, do you expect me to believe you brought these sensitive documents through Russian and American customs without a problem and that you can produce them at will?"

"Believe it! I have connections in Russian customs and being a photojournalist—my profession—I was able to bring those records into America without raising any suspicion. The customs officer didn't know what he was looking at anyway. I just said I was studying research documents in my native language and he bought it."

"When you phoned were you really in Ukraine?"

"Yes, my last job before vacation. Now let's get back to the payout."

"Well, obviously I don't have that kind of money lying around the house."

"Obviously."

"I'll need a few days to get it."

"A few days," Vitali's smug expression darkened into an uncertain frown, "why not tomorrow?"

"You don't just pull a million out of the bank without sounding alarm bells. I'll take so much from one bank and so much from another in increments. You'll have the money in a few days. How do I get in touch with you?"

"Clever...clever..." The smug countenance returned. "You don't get in touch with me. I get in touch with you."

"So you'll bring me the records when—"

"I won't carry them on me. I'm not chancing any unpleasant surprises. After I get paid I'll mail them to you."

"How do I know you won't keep them and blackmail me again later?"

"You don't know. That's just a risk you'll have to take. What you *do know* is that I'll peddle them to the highest bidder if you don't pay me. I'll bet many tabloids like the *National Enquirer* for instance would be interested in evidence of Patton's *murder*."

"All right." I shrugged in resignation. "I'll see you get what's coming to you."

✗   ✗   ✗   ✗

After this meeting, Vitali called me every night at nine p.m. sharp. On the fourth night I told him, "Come on up. Everything's ready."

Vitali arrived looking exactly as he did the first time we met. When he sat down I said, "No change of costume?"

"Nah, I'm a hipster through and through."

"You pass for one. How come you speak English so well? Not even a trace of an accent."

"English as a second language was a requirement of my schooling. Besides, I was an exchange student, learned all your slang right here in New York City."

"You learned well."

"Enough chit chat, Mr. Wells. Where's the money?"

"Everything you need is right behind you."

"Behind—" When he turned his head his jaw literally dropped at the sight of the two men in dark suits who entered silently from the hall and were staring at him. One was rather large with a face that exhibited visible dents and breaks that perfectly matched his menacing scowl. The other was handsome and young and sported a rather sly smile. Vitali's voice dropped to a shocked rasp, "Who the hell are you guys?"

The big man answered, "We're a mirage. We're nobodies. Just like you."

The handsome one laughed as Vitali turned back to me and said, "What is this? Who are they?"

The big man reiterated, "We don't exist and you'll soon join us."

Handsome intoned, "Pretty soon you won't exist either."

"Vitali," I said, "you're very clever but not too smart. After your first phone call I informed my government friends of your digital readout on my land line and they pinpointed the pay phone you were using. If you were smart you would have used different phones for each call. You were watched on the night of the second call—which was tapped by the way—and followed back to your lodgings. If I'm not mistaken, your tiny studio rental on St. Marks Place is being ransacked right now."

"Wha—you can't—I have rights—"

Visible beads of sweat formed on his brow and it seemed his complexion was a shade lighter now than when he first came in. I said, "In this age of terrorism, what with the Homeland Security Act and all, I think these gentlemen can do whatever they want to do."

Vitali's eyelids began to quiver and his upper body started to tremble. His voice hit a high pitch as he looked toward the men and said, "This man killed General Patton! I can prove it."

"Wrong—wrong—wrong!" I said. "I tried to save the general."

"Save him." His breath came in bursts as his head swiveled back to me. "You shot him!"

"Wrong again. I had a Russian grandmother who lived across the river in Brooklyn. She belonged to the Russian Orthodox Cathedral of the Transfiguration that borders Greenpoint and Williamsburg by McCarren Park. My wife—then girlfriend—loved Nana, as we called her. Once they got to know each other, Nana explained the horrors that she saw under Stalinist Communism and those stories opened Megan's eyes to the truth. Furthermore, Nana introduced her to a Russian priest who gave first hand accounts of religious oppression and life in the *gulag*. While she leaned toward agnosticism and was still resentful of what she felt was second class status for women in the various Christian churches, she was sensitive to all injustice and quickly became rabidly anti-communist, turning against the party. Our combined senses of adventure—remember we were only sixteen—made us decide to become spies. I contacted the FBI, and Megan and I both reported on party doings.

"Meanwhile, we were each respected by our *comrades* as loyal members. When Hitler invaded Russia I was ordered to join the *good fight.* And so I did while Megan allegedly served the party at home. My duties to communism were supposedly suspended while I fought in the war. The Office of Strategic Services was informed of my background by the FBI and I was told by an OSS chief never to inform the military about my clandestine activities unless a dire emergency arose because of the possibility of damaging security leaks.

"Once the war drew down party members contacted me. I learned in time that my expertise as a rifleman was an asset they could use. Before I came into play, several others tried to set General Patton up but nothing worked. After Patton liberated me and then chose me as an aide, they felt they had their best bet. I went along with the program hoping to expose them once I knew their complete plan. By the time I learned the details of this assassination scheme I couldn't return to base and warn the general because my communist superiors insisted I stay in their safe house until the hour of the deadly event.

"I accepted a Russian air rifle—copied after the British Webley—and their wood bullets. Earlier, at the party's request—the whys of which were never explained to me—I had asked for and received a few days leave, which coincided with the general's pheasant hunt. Apparently some mole was feeding the Russians his schedule. Now on that fateful day I had a gut feeling there might be more than one assassin deployed because communists trust no one. And I was right. Instead of shooting the general as ordered, I scoured the countryside in the vicinity of where I was to squeeze the trigger and I came across another marksman equipped with air rifle and wood bullets. I later discovered he was a Russian infantry sniper. The general's car was making that fateful turn as I jumped him from behind. But although I spoiled his aim, my action came an instant too late. He fired and hit the general in the neck instead of the temple as the car and truck collided. We grappled—I wanted to bring him back alive for interrogation—but he pulled a knife and ended up falling on it as we fought.

"I reported back to the base and they recovered and disposed of the body. After a grueling debriefing, first by the military brass then by the OSS, I was cleared of all wrongdoing. Meantime, the general was taken to a hospital in Heidelberg where he died of a pulmonary embolism twelve days later. Many believed his demise was aided by some Communist-leaning medical personnel. But nothing could ever be proved. I was allowed to return to my spying and accepted the credit from the Communist Party for shooting General Patton. The sniper's body was disposed of by the American military and as you correctly stated, Vitali, the Communist bosses thought he switched sides and betrayed the cause."

My rather long-winded soliloquy was interrupted by the ringing of a cell phone. It belonged to the handsome agent who answered it, listened a moment, closed the phone and said, "Well…well, Mr. Vitali Darahofsky, that's some cache of evidence you have—um— had stashed in that studio. My colleague who is fluent in Russian tells me it's a veritable treasure trove of America's traitors. Seems like you were really planning on cashing in on your visit to our great nation. Thank you for the info. Cuff him."

"Yes, sir." The big man said, "Stand up and put your hands behind your back. Do it!"

Now my original feelings of loss and anguish completely vanished, replaced with the peace and elation of philosophizing how *Old Blood and Guts* still seemed to be serving his country from beyond the grave by outing turncoats through the doings of this young Russian hoodlum. Vitali tried to speak but his mutterings were incomprehensible as his puckered mouth seemed to be gasping for air. I shook my head while they applied the cuffs. Then I said, "You tried to cash in and now you're cashing out. Goodbye Vitali."

I knew that neither I, nor the rest of the world at large, would ever see that blackmailer again.

✗

BBC'S SHERLOCK: A REVIEW

by Carole Buggé

It's no wonder Season Three of the BBC series *Sherlock* is the most watched British television series in eleven years. It's dangerously close to being a masterpiece. I viewed the first episode with the kind of breathless excitement I felt as a child watching my favorite shows, in the bygone days before VCRs, Tivo, and DVDs—when you actually had to pay attention to what was on the screen.

After Granada Television's terrific series starring Jeremy Brett as a moody, deeply neurotic Holmes, it was hard to imagine a more satisfying film version of Doyle's classic original. Just as Basil Rathbone seemed the right choice to play Holmes during Britain's war-torn years, Brett's fidgety, restless detective felt like the perfect Holmes for our time, with Edward Hardwicke's appealing, compassionate Watson as his ideal counterpoint. Hardwicke's Watson was no fool *à la* Nigel Bruce, but an intelligent, thoughtful professional who fully understood his brilliant friend's many downsides, and stood by him, anyway. At times you felt that without his Watson, Brett's Holmes would have collapsed into a cocaine-fueled stupor.

The production values were impeccable, and the Granada adaptations of Doyle's stories were often improvements on the originals, at least for the purposes of filming. The list of guest stars was a Who's Who of popular British television actors, from John Thaw to Cheryl Campbell. Patrick Gowers's music boasted a sly, twisting violin solo with a chromatic melody conjuring both the elegance and decadence of the Victorian era. The Granada series felt like the definitive reimagining of Doyle's indelible characters—until now.

Arthur Conan Doyle did not invent the detective story, but he might as well have. When Sherlock Holmes burst onto the scene in *A Study in Scarlet,* memoirs of real life detectives such as Edinburgh's James McLevy had steadily increased in popularity. Doyle was no doubt aware of them, and certainly was familiar with the work of Edgar Allan Poe, as well as *The Moonstone,* by Wilkie Collins, often regarded as the first mystery novel.

But in Sherlock Holmes, Doyle created a character for the ages, in spite of his own famously ambiguous attitude toward his celebrated detective. Gifted with astonishing powers of perception and analytical acumen, Sherlock Holmes was the first Victorian superhero. It is ironic that, given the Victorians' obsessive superstition and mysticism, their most iconic fictional character is devoted to science and reason.

Sherlock is true to the spirit of Doyle's original, and then some. Take the opener of Season Three, *The Empty Hearse*. Beginning with the play on words even a casual Holmesian would recognize, the episode is chock-a-block with a dizzying array of references, in-jokes, and homages to Conan Doyle's stories. (In more than one review of *Sherlock*, the word "canonical" appears, a sacred concept to many devoted Doyle fans.) *Sherlock* burst out of the starting gate in 2010 like a finicky filly, full of surprises and energy and juice. The success of the show isn't reducible to any one element any more than *War and Peace* can be said to be a masterpiece because it contains one of the great love stories in Russian literature. It does, but there's so much more to chew on. There are so many pleasures in *Sherlock,* it's hard to know where to begin.

The casting is as good a place as any. There is Benedict Cumberbatch as Holmes, with his improbable and sudden leap from goofy character actor to quirky leading man and teen heartthrob (cf. my niece Kylie). Appearing opposite him we have the self-effacing charm of Martin Freeman, who, as a friend of mine put it, is having "a hell of a year." In addition to playing Watson to Cumberbatch's Holmes, he is, of course, starring as Bilbo Baggins in yet another CGI-infused Peter Jackson version of Tolkien. The chemistry between the two men is terrific—and let's face it, the Holmes/Watson relationship is one of literature's great love stories. Speaking of love stories, Holmes fans (cf. real life Baker Street Irregulars) figure prominently in several episodes of *Sherlock* (which is reminiscent of the key role science fiction fans play in the delightfully quirky *Galaxy Quest*).

The cast is further graced by the presence of the wonderful Rupert Graves as Lestrade, as well as Amanda Abingdon, Freeman's real life partner, in the role of Mrs. Watson. Fresh-faced

Andrew Scott is an odd choice for Doyle's cadaverous Professor Moriarty, though his performance captures the megalomania of the mad genius. The show's co-creator Mark Gatiss is a perfectly superior, dismissive Mycroft Holmes. Una Stubbs is adorable as Mrs. Hudson, with a past amusingly racier than Doyle's original. Louise Brealey is particularly good as nerdy but clever scientist Molly Hooper, who is both in love with Holmes and onto him. In a satisfying scene in *The Empty Hearse*, she slaps him silly for his callousness toward other people's feelings.

We are told more than once that Sherlock is a "high-functioning sociopath" (sadly, many sociopaths are indeed high functioning, in positions of political, economic, and social power)—but Cumberbatch plays him as a rather appealing genius somewhere on the Asperger end of the autism spectrum. He understands other people have feelings, but lacks the emotional range or imagination to use that knowledge to his advantage. And Cumberbatch's face has the protean ability to appear both boyish and aquiline, handsome and homely. (It's a pity he was cast as Khan in the recent Star Trek prequel—even without the pointy ears, he looks exactly like a Vulcan.)

What's thrilling about the show isn't Benedict Cumberbatch's cheekbones (though my niece would argue the point), or even the series's pitch perfect balance between ominous and wryly humorous. It isn't even the clever way the edifice of the episodes have been carefully laid upon the structure of the old stories, resulting in something new and revealing and edgy. What prevents *Sherlock* from sinking under the weight of its own hipness is the combination of all these elements, as well as the sly, tongue-in-cheek tone and masterful editing that makes the viewer feel just as Doyle's readers must have felt—always one step behind a brilliance that is challenging, bracing, and a little disturbing.

The way the show handles the dichotomies of its characters is mirrored by its managing to be a respectful homage to Conan Doyle's original, as well as a fresh reimagining for our digital world. In *Sherlock,* Holmes uses digital devices, social media, and texting much the way Doyle's character used newspapers, obscure monographs, and police blotters. The show's creators merge the old and new so seamlessly the viewer experiences a little *frisson* of pleasure at the sight of Cumberbatch on his knees, nose to the ground, peering through a magnifying glass to scour the crime scene for clues. High tech is all well and good, but sometimes the old tools do the job.

And it is a tribute to *Sherlock* that it straddles the often uncomfortable blend of the old and new with such apparent effortlessness. For hard core Sherlockians, who can be demanding, the iconic images have been lovingly preserved: besides the magnifying glass, there is the deerstalker hat, the bullet holes in the parlor wall, the homemade chemistry lab—complete with contemporary, often humorous explanations. The Inverness cape made famous in Sidney Paget's illustrations even makes an appearance in one episode, though for the most part it has been replaced by a long, flowing wool coat, but Cumberbatch looks dashing enough in it.

Even the show's music is impressive. The driving opening theme, a gypsy-infused 6/8 melody in a minor key, manages to sound both jaunty and dangerous. David Arnold and Michael Price aren't the first composers to use the cimbalom (an Eastern European version of a hammered dulcimer) in a Holmes project. The instrument appears in Han Zimmer's score for the forgettable Robert Downey movies (cf. Holmes Spinoffs Not Worth Mentioning), as well as *Sherlock Holmes and the Secret Weapon,* the fourth Rathbone/Bruce vehicle, released in 1942, featuring Holmes and Watson fighting Nazis during World War II. Arnold and Price's music hints at something dark and exotic about Sherlock Holmes, perhaps suggesting roots in the murky, mysterious Balkans. (Doyle's Holmes had a grandmother who was the sister of the French artist Vernet, a source of endless speculation among Sherlockians.)

True, the series has its uneven patches. The second episode of Season One didn't quite recapitulate the wonder of the first, but it came back strong in Episode Three. The closer of the third season, *His Last Vow*, featuring the pernicious blackmailer Charles Magnusson, is not stellar. Presumably they changed the name from Doyle's original, wonderfully Dickensian "Milverton" to accommodate Danish actor Lars Mikkelsen, (fresh from Denmark's astonishingly brilliant *Borgen*), but it's a pity, nonetheless. The plot is jerky and unconvincing, there are too many unanswered questions and inexplicable moments, and character motivations are oddly thin. The big "reveal" about Mrs. Watson's past feels shallow and too much like something you'd see on "24" or "NCIS," or even, God forbid, "Elementary." (cf. Not So Successful Holmes Spin-Offs.)

But even for an alien plunked down on planet Earth with no previous acquaintance with the works of Conan Doyle, his many imitators, spin offs, and heirs (cf. Adrian Monk and Gregory House), *Sherlock* is, quite simply, kick ass. Witty, urbane, and original, it is the most brilliantly conceived, written, and directed series to come out of the UK in a long time. After slogging through yet another stately, soap-opera inspired episode of *Downton Abbey* (cf. "Die, Bates, Die!"), I can hardly wait for the next episode of *Sherlock*.

✗

THE ADVENTURE OF THE BLUE CARBUNCLE

by Arthur Conan Doyle

I had called upon my friend Sherlock Holmes upon the second morning after Christmas, with the intention of wishing him the compliments of the season. He was lounging upon the sofa in a purple dressing-gown, a pipe-rack within his reach upon the right, and a pile of crumpled morning papers, evidently newly studied, near at hand. Beside the couch was a wooden chair, and on the angle of the back hung a very seedy and disreputable hard-felt hat, much the worse for wear, and cracked in several places. A lens and a forceps lying upon the seat of the chair suggested that the hat had been suspended in this manner for the purpose of examination.

"You are engaged," said I; "perhaps I interrupt you."

"Not at all. I am glad to have a friend with whom I can discuss my results. The matter is a perfectly trivial one"—he jerked his thumb in the direction of the old hat—"but there are points in connection with it which are not entirely devoid of interest and even of instruction."

I seated myself in his armchair and warmed my hands before his crackling fire, for a sharp frost had set in, and the windows were thick with the ice crystals. "I suppose," I remarked, "that, homely as it looks, this thing has some deadly story linked on to it—that it is the clue which will guide you in the solution of some mystery and the punishment of some crime."

"No, no. No crime," said Sherlock Holmes, laughing. "Only one of those whimsical little incidents which will happen when you have four million human beings all jostling each other within the space of a few square miles. Amid the action and reaction of so dense a swarm of humanity, every possible combination of events may be expected to take place, and many a little problem will be presented which may be striking and bizarre without being criminal. We have already had experience of such."

"So much so," I remarked, "that of the last six cases which I have added to my notes, three have been entirely free of any legal crime."

"Precisely. You allude to my attempt to recover the Irene Adler papers, to the singular case of Miss Mary Sutherland, and to the adventure of the man with the twisted lip. Well, I have no doubt that this small matter will fall into the same innocent category. You know Peterson, the commissionaire?"

"Yes."

"It is to him that this trophy belongs."

"It is his hat."

"No, no, he found it. Its owner is unknown. I beg that you will look upon it not as a battered billycock but as an intellectual problem. And, first, as to how it came here. It arrived upon Christmas morning, in company with a good fat goose, which is, I have no doubt, roasting at this moment in front of Peterson's fire. The facts are these: about four o'clock on Christmas morning, Peterson, who, as you know, is a very honest fellow, was returning from some small jollification and was making his way homeward down Tottenham Court Road. In front of him he saw, in the gaslight, a tallish man, walking with a slight stagger, and carrying a white goose slung over his shoulder. As he reached the corner of Goodge Street, a row broke out between this stranger and a little knot of roughs. One of the latter knocked off the man's hat, on which he raised his stick to defend himself and, swinging it over his head, smashed the shop window behind him. Peterson had rushed forward to protect the stranger from his assailants; but the man, shocked at having broken the window, and seeing an official-looking person in uniform rushing towards him, dropped his goose, took to his heels, and vanished amid the labyrinth of small streets which lie at the back of Tottenham Court Road. The roughs had also fled at the appearance of Peterson, so that he was left in possession of the field of battle, and also of the spoils of victory in the shape of this battered hat and a most unimpeachable Christmas goose."

"Which surely he restored to their owner?"

"My dear fellow, there lies the problem. It is true that 'For Mrs. Henry Baker' was printed upon a small card which was tied to the bird's left leg, and it is also true that the initials 'H. B.' are legible upon the lining of this hat, but as there are some thousands of

Bakers, and some hundreds of Henry Bakers in this city of ours, it is not easy to restore lost property to any one of them."

"What, then, did Peterson do?"

"He brought round both hat and goose to me on Christmas morning, knowing that even the smallest problems are of interest to me. The goose we retained until this morning, when there were signs that, in spite of the slight frost, it would be well that it should be eaten without unnecessary delay. Its finder has carried it off, therefore, to fulfil the ultimate destiny of a goose, while I continue to retain the hat of the unknown gentleman who lost his Christmas dinner."

"Did he not advertise?"

"No."

"Then, what clue could you have as to his identity?"

"Only as much as we can deduce."

"From his hat?"

"Precisely."

"But you are joking. What can you gather from this old battered felt?"

"Here is my lens. You know my methods. What can you gather yourself as to the individuality of the man who has worn this article?"

I took the tattered object in my hands and turned it over rather ruefully. It was a very ordinary black hat of the usual round shape, hard and much the worse for wear. The lining had been of red silk, but was a good deal discoloured. There was no maker's name; but, as Holmes had remarked, the initials "H. B." were scrawled upon one side. It was pierced in the brim for a hat-securer, but the elastic was missing. For the rest, it was cracked, exceedingly dusty, and spotted in several places, although there seemed to have been some attempt to hide the discoloured patches by smearing them with ink.

"I can see nothing," said I, handing it back to my friend.

"On the contrary, Watson, you can see everything. You fail, however, to reason from what you see. You are too timid in drawing your inferences."

"Then, pray tell me what it is that you can infer from this hat?"

He picked it up and gazed at it in the peculiar introspective fashion which was characteristic of him. "It is perhaps less suggestive than it might have been," he remarked, "and yet there are a few inferences which are very distinct, and a few others which represent at least a strong balance of probability. That the man was highly intellectual is of course obvious upon the face of it, and also that he was fairly well-to-do within the last three years, although he has now fallen upon evil days. He had foresight, but has less now than formerly, pointing to a moral retrogression, which, when taken with the decline of his fortunes, seems to indicate some evil influence, probably drink, at work upon him. This may account also for the obvious fact that his wife has ceased to love him."

"My dear Holmes!"

"He has, however, retained some degree of self-respect," he continued, disregarding my remonstrance. "He is a man who leads a sedentary life, goes out little, is out of training entirely, is middle-aged, has grizzled hair which he has had cut within the last few days, and which he anoints with lime-cream. These are the more patent facts which are to be deduced from his hat. Also, by the way, that it is extremely improbable that he has gas laid on in his house."

"You are certainly joking, Holmes."

"Not in the least. Is it possible that even now, when I give you these results, you are unable to see how they are attained?"

"I have no doubt that I am very stupid, but I must confess that I am unable to follow you. For example, how did you deduce that this man was intellectual?"

For answer Holmes clapped the hat upon his head. It came right over the forehead and settled upon the bridge of his nose. "It is a question of cubic capacity," said he; "a man with so large a brain must have something in it."

"The decline of his fortunes, then?"

"This hat is three years old. These flat brims curled at the edge came in then. It is a hat of the very best quality. Look at the band of ribbed silk and the excellent lining. If this man could afford to buy so expensive a hat three years ago, and has had no hat since, then he has assuredly gone down in the world."

"Well, that is clear enough, certainly. But how about the foresight and the moral retrogression?"

Sherlock Holmes laughed. "Here is the foresight," said he putting his finger upon the little disc and loop of the hat-securer. "They are never sold upon hats. If this man ordered one, it is a sign of a certain amount of foresight, since he went out of his way to take this precaution against the wind. But since we see that he has broken the elastic and has not troubled to replace it, it is obvious that he has less foresight now than formerly, which is a distinct proof of a weakening nature. On the other hand, he has endeavoured to conceal some of these stains upon the felt by daubing them with ink, which is a sign that he has not entirely lost his self-respect."

"Your reasoning is certainly plausible."

"The further points, that he is middle-aged, that his hair is grizzled, that it has been recently cut, and that he uses lime-cream, are all to be gathered from a close examination of the lower part of the lining. The lens discloses a large number of hair-ends, clean cut by the scissors of the barber. They all appear to be adhesive, and there is a distinct odour of lime-cream. This dust, you will observe, is not the gritty, grey dust of the street but the fluffy brown dust of the house, showing that it has been hung up indoors most of the time, while the marks of moisture upon the inside are proof positive that the wearer perspired very freely, and could therefore, hardly be in the best of training."

"But his wife—you said that she had ceased to love him."

"This hat has not been brushed for weeks. When I see you, my dear Watson, with a week's accumulation of dust upon your hat, and when your wife allows you to go out in such a state, I shall fear that you also have been unfortunate enough to lose your wife's affection."

"But he might be a bachelor."

"Nay, he was bringing home the goose as a peace-offering to his wife. Remember the card upon the bird's leg."

"You have an answer to everything. But how on earth do you deduce that the gas is not laid on in his house?"

"One tallow stain, or even two, might come by chance; but when I see no less than five, I think that there can be little doubt that the individual must be brought into frequent contact with burning tallow—walks upstairs at night probably with his hat in one hand and a guttering candle in the other. Anyhow, he never got tallow-stains from a gas-jet. Are you satisfied?"

"Well, it is very ingenious," said I, laughing; "but since, as you said just now, there has been no crime committed, and no harm done save the loss of a goose, all this seems to be rather a waste of energy."

Sherlock Holmes had opened his mouth to reply, when the door flew open, and Peterson, the commissionaire, rushed into the apartment with flushed cheeks and the face of a man who is dazed with astonishment.

"The goose, Mr. Holmes! The goose, sir!" he gasped.

"Eh? What of it, then? Has it returned to life and flapped off through the kitchen window?" Holmes twisted himself round upon the sofa to get a fairer view of the man's excited face.

"See here, sir! See what my wife found in its crop!" He held out his hand and displayed upon the centre of the palm a brilliantly scintillating blue stone, rather smaller than a bean in size, but of such purity and radiance that it twinkled like an electric point in the dark hollow of his hand.

Sherlock Holmes sat up with a whistle. "By Jove, Peterson!" said he, "this is treasure trove indeed. I suppose you know what you have got?"

"A diamond, sir? A precious stone. It cuts into glass as though it were putty."

"It's more than a precious stone. It is *the* precious stone."

"Not the Countess of Morcar's blue carbuncle!" I ejaculated.

"Precisely so. I ought to know its size and shape, seeing that I have read the advertisement about it in *The Times* every day lately. It is absolutely unique, and its value can only be conjectured, but the reward offered of £1000 is certainly not within a twentieth part of the market price."

"A thousand pounds! Great Lord of mercy!" The commissionaire plumped down into a chair and stared from one to the other of us.

"That is the reward, and I have reason to know that there are sentimental considerations in the background which would induce the Countess to part with half her fortune if she could but recover the gem."

"It was lost, if I remember aright, at the Hotel Cosmopolitan," I remarked.

"Precisely so, on December 22nd, just five days ago. John Horner, a plumber, was accused of having abstracted it from the lady's jewel-case. The evidence against him was so strong that the case has been referred to the Assizes. I have some account of the matter here, I believe." He rummaged amid his newspapers, glancing over the dates, until at last he smoothed one out, doubled it over, and read the following paragraph:

"Hotel Cosmopolitan Jewel Robbery. John Horner, 26, plumber, was brought up upon the charge of having upon the 22nd inst., abstracted from the jewel-case of the Countess of Morcar the valuable gem known as the blue carbuncle. James Ryder, upper-attendant at the hotel, gave his evidence to the effect that he had shown Horner up to the dressing-room of the Countess of Morcar upon the day of the robbery in order that he might solder the second bar of the grate, which was loose. He had remained with Horner some little time, but had finally been called away. On returning, he found that Horner had disappeared, that the bureau had been forced open, and that the small morocco casket in which, as it afterwards transpired, the Countess was accustomed to keep her jewel, was lying empty upon the dressing-table. Ryder instantly gave the alarm, and Horner was arrested the same evening; but the stone could not be found either upon his person or in his rooms. Catherine Cusack, maid to the Countess, deposed to having heard Ryder's cry of dismay on discovering the robbery, and to having rushed into the room, where she found matters as described by the last witness. Inspector Bradstreet, B division, gave evidence as to the arrest of Horner, who struggled frantically, and protested his innocence in the strongest terms. Evidence of a previous conviction for robbery having been given against the prisoner, the magistrate refused to deal summarily with the offence, but referred it to the Assizes. Horner, who had shown signs of intense emotion during the proceedings, fainted away at the conclusion and was carried out of court."

"Hum! So much for the police-court," said Holmes thoughtfully, tossing aside the paper. "The question for us now to solve is the sequence of events leading from a rifled jewel-case at one end to the crop of a goose in Tottenham Court Road at the other. You see, Watson, our little deductions have suddenly assumed a much more important and less innocent aspect. Here is the stone; the stone came from the goose, and the goose came from Mr. Henry Baker, the gentleman with the bad hat and all the other characteristics with which I have bored you. So now we must set ourselves very seriously to finding this gentleman and ascertaining what part he has played in this little mystery. To do this, we must try the simplest means first, and these lie undoubtedly in an advertisement in all the evening papers. If this fail, I shall have recourse to other methods."

"What will you say?"

"Give me a pencil and that slip of paper. Now, then: 'Found at the corner of Goodge Street, a goose and a black felt hat. Mr. Henry Baker can have the same by applying at 6:30 this evening at 221B, Baker Street.' That is clear and concise."

"Very. But will he see it?"

"Well, he is sure to keep an eye on the papers, since, to a poor man, the loss was a heavy one. He was clearly so scared by his mischance in breaking the window and by the approach of Peterson that he thought of nothing but flight, but since then he must have bitterly regretted the impulse which caused him to drop his bird. Then, again, the introduction of his name will cause him to see it, for everyone who knows him will direct his attention to it. Here you are, Peterson, run down to the advertising agency and have this put in the evening papers."

"In which, sir?"

"Oh, in the *Globe, Star, Pall Mall, St. James's, Evening News, Standard, Echo,* and any others that occur to you."

"Very well, sir. And this stone?"

"Ah, yes, I shall keep the stone. Thank you. And, I say, Peterson, just buy a goose on your way back and leave it here with me, for we must have one to give to this gentleman in place of the one which your family is now devouring."

When the commissionaire had gone, Holmes took up the stone and held it against the light. "It's a bonny thing," said he. "Just see how it glints and sparkles. Of course it is a nucleus and focus of crime. Every good stone is. They are the devil's pet baits. In the larger and older jewels every facet may stand for a bloody deed. This stone is not yet twenty years old. It was found in the banks of the Amoy River in southern China and is remarkable in having every characteristic of the carbuncle, save that it is blue in shade instead of ruby red. In spite of its youth, it has already a sinister history. There have been two murders, a vitriol-throwing, a suicide, and several robberies brought about for the sake of this forty-grain weight of crystallised charcoal. Who would think that so pretty a toy would be a purveyor to the gallows and the prison? I'll lock it up in my strong box now and drop a line to the Countess to say that we have it."

"Do you think that this man Horner is innocent?"

"I cannot tell."

"Well, then, do you imagine that this other one, Henry Baker, had anything to do with the matter?"

"It is, I think, much more likely that Henry Baker is an absolutely innocent man, who had no idea that the bird which he was carrying was of considerably more value than if it were made of solid gold. That, however, I shall determine by a very simple test if we have an answer to our advertisement."

"And you can do nothing until then?"

"Nothing."

"In that case I shall continue my professional round. But I shall come back in the evening at the hour you have mentioned, for I should like to see the solution of so tangled a business."

"Very glad to see you. I dine at seven. There is a woodcock, I believe. By the way, in view of recent occurrences, perhaps I ought to ask Mrs. Hudson to examine its crop."

I had been delayed at a case, and it was a little after half-past six when I found myself in Baker Street once more. As I approached the house I saw a tall man in a Scotch bonnet with a coat which was buttoned up to his chin waiting outside in the bright semicircle which was thrown from the fanlight. Just as I arrived the door was opened, and we were shown up together to Holmes' room.

"Mr. Henry Baker, I believe," said he, rising from his armchair and greeting his visitor with the easy air of geniality which he could so readily assume. "Pray take this chair by the fire, Mr. Baker. It is a cold night, and I observe that your circulation is more adapted for summer than for winter. Ah, Watson, you have just come at the right time. Is that your hat, Mr. Baker?"

"Yes, sir, that is undoubtedly my hat."

He was a large man with rounded shoulders, a massive head, and a broad, intelligent face, sloping down to a pointed beard of grizzled brown. A touch of red in nose and cheeks, with a slight tremour of his extended hand, recalled Holmes's surmise as to his habits. His rusty black frock-coat was buttoned right up in front, with the collar turned up, and his lank wrists protruded from his sleeves without a sign of cuff or shirt. He spoke in a slow staccato fashion, choosing his words with care, and gave the impression generally of a man of learning and letters who had had ill-usage at the hands of fortune.

"We have retained these things for some days," said Holmes, "because we expected to see an advertisement from you giving your address. I am at a loss to know now why you did not advertise."

Our visitor gave a rather shamefaced laugh. "Shillings have not been so plentiful with me as they once were," he remarked. "I had no doubt that the gang of roughs who assaulted me had carried off both my hat and the bird. I did not care to spend more money in a hopeless attempt at recovering them."

"Very naturally. By the way, about the bird, we were compelled to eat it."

"To eat it!" Our visitor half rose from his chair in his excitement.

"Yes, it would have been of no use to anyone had we not done so. But I presume that this other goose upon the sideboard, which is about the same weight and perfectly fresh, will answer your purpose equally well?"

"Oh, certainly, certainly," answered Mr. Baker with a sigh of relief.

"Of course, we still have the feathers, legs, crop, and so on of your own bird, so if you wish—"

The man burst into a hearty laugh. "They might be useful to me as relics of my adventure," said he, "but beyond that I can hardly see what use the *disjecta membra* of my late acquaintance are going to be to me. No, sir, I think that, with your permission, I will confine my attentions to the excellent bird which I perceive upon the sideboard."

Sherlock Holmes glanced sharply across at me with a slight shrug of his shoulders.

"There is your hat, then, and there your bird," said he. "By the way, would it bore you to tell me where you got the other one from? I am somewhat of a fowl fancier, and I have seldom seen a better grown goose."

"Certainly, sir," said Baker, who had risen and tucked his newly gained property under his arm. "There are a few of us who frequent the Alpha Inn, near the Museum—we are to be found in the Museum itself during the day, you understand. This year our good host, Windigate by name, instituted a goose club, by which, on consideration of some few pence every week, we were each to receive a bird at Christmas. My pence were duly paid, and the rest is familiar to you. I am much indebted to you, sir, for a Scotch bonnet is fitted neither to my years nor my gravity." With a comical pomposity of manner he bowed solemnly to both of us and strode off upon his way.

"So much for Mr Henry Baker," said Holmes when he had closed the door behind him. "It is quite certain that he knows nothing whatever about the matter. Are you hungry, Watson?"

"Not particularly."

"Then I suggest that we turn our dinner into a supper and follow up this clue while it is still hot."

"By all means."

It was a bitter night, so we drew on our ulsters and wrapped cravats about our throats. Outside, the stars were shining coldly in a cloudless sky, and the breath of the passers-by blew out into smoke like so many pistol shots. Our footfalls rang out crisply and loudly as we swung through the doctors's quarter, Wimpole Street, Harley Street, and so through Wigmore Street into Oxford Street. In a quarter of an hour we were in Bloomsbury at the Alpha Inn, which is a small public-house at the corner of one of the streets which runs down into Holborn. Holmes pushed open the door of the private bar and ordered two glasses of beer from the ruddy-faced, white-aproned landlord.

"Your beer should be excellent if it is as good as your geese," said he.

"My geese!" The man seemed surprised.

"Yes. I was speaking only half an hour ago to Mr Henry Baker, who was a member of your goose club."

"Ah! yes, I see. But you see, sir, them's not *our* geese."

"Indeed! Whose, then?"

"Well, I got the two dozen from a salesman in Covent Garden."

"Indeed? I know some of them. Which was it?"

"Breckinridge is his name."

"Ah! I don't know him. Well, here's your good health landlord, and prosperity to your house. Good-night."

"Now for Mr Breckinridge," he continued, buttoning up his coat as we came out into the frosty air. "Remember, Watson that though we have so homely a thing as a goose at one end of this chain, we have at the other a man who will certainly get seven years's penal servitude unless we can establish his innocence. It is possible that our inquiry may but confirm his guilt; but, in any case, we have a line of investigation which has been missed by the police, and which a singular chance has placed in our hands. Let us follow it out to the bitter end. Faces to the south, then, and quick march!"

We passed across Holborn, down Endell Street, and so through a zigzag of slums to Covent Garden Market. One of the largest stalls bore the name of Breckinridge upon it, and the proprietor a horsey-looking man, with a sharp face and trim side-whiskers was helping a boy to put up the shutters.

"Good-evening. It's a cold night," said Holmes.

The salesman nodded and shot a questioning glance at my companion.

"Sold out of geese, I see," continued Holmes, pointing at the bare slabs of marble.

"Let you have five hundred to-morrow morning."

"That's no good."

"Well, there are some on the stall with the gas-flare."

"Ah, but I was recommended to you."

"Who by?"

"The landlord of the Alpha."

"Oh, yes; I sent him a couple of dozen."

"Fine birds they were, too. Now where did you get them from?"

To my surprise the question provoked a burst of anger from the salesman.

"Now, then, mister," said he, with his head cocked and his arms akimbo, "what are you driving at? Let's have it straight, now."

"It is straight enough. I should like to know who sold you the geese which you supplied to the Alpha."

"Well then, I shan't tell you. So now!"

"Oh, it is a matter of no importance; but I don't know why you should be so warm over such a trifle."

"Warm! You'd be as warm, maybe, if you were as pestered as I am. When I pay good money for a good article there should be an end of the business; but it's 'Where are the geese?' and 'Who did you sell the geese to?' and 'What will you take for the geese?' One would think they were the only geese in the world, to hear the fuss that is made over them."

"Well, I have no connection with any other people who have been making inquiries," said Holmes carelessly. "If you won't tell us the bet is off, that is all. But I'm always ready to back my opinion on a matter of fowls, and I have a fiver on it that the bird I ate is country bred."

"Well, then, you've lost your fiver, for it's town bred," snapped the salesman.

"It's nothing of the kind."

"I say it is."

"I don't believe it."

"D'you think you know more about fowls than I, who have handled them ever since I was a nipper? I tell you, all those birds that went to the Alpha were town bred."

"You'll never persuade me to believe that."

"Will you bet, then?"

"It's merely taking your money, for I know that I am right. But I'll have a sovereign on with you, just to teach you not to be obstinate."

The salesman chuckled grimly. "Bring me the books, Bill," said he.

The small boy brought round a small thin volume and a great greasy-backed one, laying them out together beneath the hanging lamp.

"Now then, Mr Cocksure," said the salesman, "I thought that I was out of geese, but before I finish you'll find that there is still one left in my shop. You see this little book?"

"Well?"

"That's the list of the folk from whom I buy. D'you see? Well, then, here on this page are the country folk, and the numbers after their names are where their accounts are in the big ledger. Now, then! You see this other page in red ink? Well, that is a list of my town suppliers. Now, look at that third name. Just read it out to me."

"Mrs Oakshott, 117, Brixton Road—249," read Holmes.

"Quite so. Now turn that up in the ledger."

Holmes turned to the page indicated. "Here you are, 'Mrs Oakshott, 117, Brixton Road, egg and poultry supplier.' "

"Now, then, what's the last entry?"

"'December 22nd. Twenty-four geese at 7s 6d'"

"Quite so. There you are. And underneath?"

"'Sold to Mr Windigate of the Alpha, at 12s'"

"What have you to say now?"

Sherlock Holmes looked deeply chagrined. He drew a sovereign from his pocket and threw it down upon the slab, turning away with the air of a man whose disgust is too deep for words. A few yards off he stopped under a lamp-post and laughed in the hearty, noiseless fashion which was peculiar to him.

"When you see a man with whiskers of that cut and the 'Pink 'un' protruding out of his pocket, you can always draw him by a bet," said he. "I daresay that if I had put £100 down in front of him, that man would not have given me such complete information as was drawn from him by the idea that he was doing me on a wager. Well, Watson, we are, I fancy, nearing the end of our quest, and the only point which remains to be determined is whether we should go on to this Mrs Oakshott to-night, or whether we should reserve it for to-morrow. It is clear from what that surly fellow said that there are others besides ourselves who are anxious about the matter, and I should—"

His remarks were suddenly cut short by a loud hubbub which broke out from the stall which we had just left. Turning round we saw a little rat-faced fellow standing in the centre of the circle of yellow light which was thrown by the swinging lamp, while Breckinridge, the salesman, framed in the door of his stall, was shaking his fists fiercely at the cringing figure.

"I've had enough of you and your geese," he shouted. "I wish you were all at the devil together. If you come pestering me any more with your silly talk I'll set the dog at you. You bring Mrs Oakshott here and I'll answer her, but what have you to do with it? Did I buy the geese off you?"

"No; but one of them was mine all the same," whined the little man.

"Well, then, ask Mrs Oakshott for it."

"She told me to ask you."

"Well, you can ask the King of Proosia, for all I care. I've had enough of it. Get out of this!" He rushed fiercely forward, and the inquirer flitted away into the darkness.

"Ha! this may save us a visit to Brixton Road," whispered Holmes. "Come with me, and we will see what is to be made of this fellow." Striding through the scattered knots of people who lounged round the flaring stalls, my companion speedily overtook the little man and touched him upon the shoulder. He sprang round, and I could see in the gas-light that every vestige of colour had been driven from his face.

"Who are you, then? What do you want?" he asked in a quavering voice.

"You will excuse me," said Holmes blandly, "but I could not help overhearing the questions which you put to the salesman just now. I think that I could be of assistance to you."

"You? Who are you? How could you know anything of the matter?"

"My name is Sherlock Holmes. It is my business to know what other people don't know."

"But you can know nothing of this?"

"Excuse me, I know everything of it. You are endeavouring to trace some geese which were sold by Mrs Oakshott, of Brixton Road, to a salesman named Breckinridge, by him in turn to Mr Windigate, of the Alpha, and by him to his club, of which Mr Henry Baker is a member."

"Oh, sir, you are the very man whom I have longed to meet," cried the little fellow with outstretched hands and quivering fingers. "I can hardly explain to you how interested I am in this matter."

Sherlock Holmes hailed a four-wheeler which was passing. "In that case we had better discuss it in a cosy room rather than in this wind-swept market-place," said he. "But pray tell me, before we go farther, who it is that I have the pleasure of assisting."

The man hesitated for an instant. "My name is John Robinson," he answered with a sidelong glance.

"No, no; the real name," said Holmes sweetly. "It is always awkward doing business with an alias."

A flush sprang to the white cheeks of the stranger. "Well then," said he, "my real name is James Ryder."

"Precisely so. Head attendant at the Hotel Cosmopolitan. Pray step into the cab, and I shall soon be able to tell you everything which you would wish to know."

The little man stood glancing from one to the other of us with half-frightened, half-hopeful eyes, as one who is not sure whether he is on the verge of a windfall or of a catastrophe. Then he stepped into the cab, and in half an hour we were back in the sitting-room at Baker Street. Nothing had been said during our drive, but the high, thin breathing of our new companion, and the claspings and unclaspings of his hands, spoke of the nervous tension within him.

"Here we are!" said Holmes cheerily as we filed into the room. "The fire looks very seasonable in this weather. You look cold, Mr Ryder. Pray take the basket-chair. I will just put on my slippers before we settle this little matter of yours. Now, then! You want to know what became of those geese?"

"Yes, sir."

"Or rather, I fancy, of that goose. It was one bird, I imagine in which you were interested—white, with a black bar across the tail."

Ryder quivered with emotion. "Oh, sir," he cried, "can you tell me where it went to?"

"It came here."

"Here?"

"Yes, and a most remarkable bird it proved. I don't wonder that you should take an interest in it. It laid an egg after it was dead— the bonniest, brightest little blue egg that ever was seen. I have it here in my museum."

Our visitor staggered to his feet and clutched the mantelpiece with his right hand. Holmes unlocked his strong-box and held up the blue carbuncle, which shone out like a star, with a cold, brilliant, many-pointed radiance. Ryder stood glaring with a drawn face, uncertain whether to claim or to disown it.

"The game's up, Ryder," said Holmes quietly. "Hold up, man, or you'll be into the fire! Give him an arm back into his chair, Watson. He's not got blood enough to go in for felony with impunity. Give him a dash of brandy. So! Now he looks a little more human. What a shrimp it is, to be sure!"

For a moment he had staggered and nearly fallen, but the brandy brought a tinge of colour into his cheeks, and he sat staring with frightened eyes at his accuser.

"I have almost every link in my hands, and all the proofs which I could possibly need, so there is little which you need tell me. Still, that little may as well be cleared up to make the case complete. You had heard, Ryder, of this blue stone of the Countess of Morcar's?"

"It was Catherine Cusack who told me of it," said he in a crackling voice.

"I see—her ladyship's waiting-maid. Well, the temptation of sudden wealth so easily acquired was too much for you, as it has been for better men before you; but you were not very scrupulous in the means you used. It seems to me, Ryder, that there is the making of a very pretty villain in you. You knew that this man Horner, the plumber, had been concerned in some such matter before, and that suspicion would rest the more readily upon him. What did you do, then? You made some small job in my lady's room—you and your confederate Cusack—and you managed that he should be the man sent for. Then, when he had left, you rifled the jewel-case, raised the alarm, and had this unfortunate man arrested. You then—"

Ryder threw himself down suddenly upon the rug and clutched at my companion's knees. "For God's sake, have mercy!" he shrieked. "Think of my father! Of my mother! It would break their hearts. I never went wrong before! I never will again. I swear it. I'll swear it on a Bible. Oh, don't bring it into court! For Christ's sake, don't!"

"Get back into your chair!" said Holmes sternly. "It is very well to cringe and crawl now, but you thought little enough of this poor Horner in the dock for a crime of which he knew nothing."

"I will fly, Mr Holmes. I will leave the country, sir. Then the charge against him will break down."

"Hum! We will talk about that. And now let us hear a true account of the next act. How came the stone into the goose, and how came the goose into the open market? Tell us the truth, for there lies your only hope of safety."

Ryder passed his tongue over his parched lips. "I will tell you it just as it happened, sir," said he. "When Horner had been arrested, it seemed to me that it would be best for me to get away with the stone at once, for I did not know at what moment the police might not take it into their heads to search me and my room. There was no place about the hotel where it would be safe. I went out, as if on some commission, and I made for my sister's house. She had married a man named Oakshott, and lived in Brixton Road, where she fattened fowls for the market. All the way there every man I met seemed to me to be a policeman or a detective; and, for all that it was a cold night, the sweat was pouring down my face before I came to the Brixton Road. My sister asked me what was the matter, and why I was so pale; but I told her that I had been upset by the jewel robbery at the hotel. Then I went into the back yard and smoked a pipe and wondered what it would be best to do.

"I had a friend once called Maudsley, who went to the bad, and has just been serving his time in Pentonville. One day he had met me, and fell into talk about the ways of thieves, and how they could get rid of what they stole. I knew that he would be true to me, for I knew one or two things about him; so I made up my mind to go right on to Kilburn, where he lived, and take him into my confidence. He would show me how to turn the stone into money. But how to get to him in safety? I thought of the agonies I had gone through in coming from the hotel. I might at any moment be seized and searched, and there would be the stone in my waistcoat pocket. I was leaning against the wall at the time and looking at the geese which were waddling about round my feet, and suddenly an idea came into my head which showed me how I could beat the best detective that ever lived.

"My sister had told me some weeks before that I might have the pick of her geese for a Christmas present, and I knew that she was always as good as her word. I would take my goose now, and in it I would carry my stone to Kilburn. There was a little shed in the yard, and behind this I drove one of the birds—a fine big one, white, with a barred tail. I caught it, and prying its bill open, I thrust the stone down its throat as far as my finger could reach. The bird gave a gulp, and I felt the stone pass along its gullet and down into its crop. But the creature flapped and struggled, and out came my sister to know what was the matter. As I turned to speak to her the brute broke loose and fluttered off among the others.

"'Whatever were you doing with that bird, Jem?' says she.

"'Well,' said I, 'you said you'd give me one for Christmas, and I was feeling which was the fattest.'

"'Oh,' says she, 'we've set yours aside for you—Jem's bird, we call it. It's the big white one over yonder. There's twenty-six of them, which makes one for you, and one for us, and two dozen for the market.'

"'Thank you, Maggie,' says I; 'but if it is all the same to you, I'd rather have that one I was handling just now.'

"'The other is a good three pound heavier,' said she, 'and we fattened it expressly for you.'

"'Never mind. I'll have the other, and I'll take it now,' said I.

"'Oh, just as you like,' said she, a little huffed. 'Which is it you want, then?'

"'That white one with the barred tail, right in the middle of the flock.'

"'Oh, very well. Kill it and take it with you.'

"Well, I did what she said, Mr Holmes, and I carried the bird all the way to Kilburn. I told my pal what I had done, for he was a man that it was easy to tell a thing like that to. He laughed until he choked, and we got a knife and opened the goose. My heart turned to water, for there was no sign of the stone, and I knew that some terrible mistake had occurred. I left the bird, rushed back to my sister's, and hurried into the back yard. There was not a bird to be seen there.

"'Where are they all, Maggie?' I cried.

"'Gone to the dealer's, Jem.'

"'Which dealer's?'

"'Breckinridge, of Covent Garden.'

"'But was there another with a barred tail?' I asked, 'the same as the one I chose?'

"'Yes, Jem; there were two barred-tailed ones, and I could never tell them apart.'

"Well, then, of course I saw it all, and I ran off as hard as my feet would carry me to this man Breckinridge; but he had sold the lot at once, and not one word would he tell me as to where they had gone. You heard him yourselves to-night. Well, he has always answered me like that. My sister thinks that I am going mad. Sometimes I think that I am myself. And now—and now I am myself a branded thief, without ever having touched the wealth for which I sold my character. God help me! God help me!" He burst into convulsive sobbing, with his face buried in his hands.

There was a long silence, broken only by his heavy breathing and by the measured tapping of Sherlock Holmes's finger-tips upon the edge of the table. Then my friend rose and threw open the door.

"Get out!" said he.

"What, sir! Oh, Heaven bless you!"

"No more words. Get out!"

And no more words were needed. There was a rush, a clatter upon the stairs, the bang of a door, and the crisp rattle of running footfalls from the street.

"After all, Watson," said Holmes, reaching up his hand for his clay pipe, "I am not retained by the police to supply their deficiencies. If Horner were in danger it would be another thing; but this fellow will not appear against him, and the case must collapse. I suppose that I am commuting a felony, but it is just possible that I am saving a soul. This fellow will not go wrong again; he is too terribly frightened. Send him to gaol now, and you make him a gaol-bird for life. Besides, it is the season of forgiveness. Chance has put in our way a most singular and whimsical problem, and its solution is its own reward. If you will have the goodness to touch the bell, Doctor, we will begin another investigation, in which, also a bird will be the chief feature."

Printed in Great Britain
by Amazon

43083568R00088